I0521415

A Fortnight of Snow
The Journey Begins

A novel by
Eddie Bean

Steele Solutions Inc.

This is a work of fiction. Names, characters, places and incidents either are the product of the author's imagination or are used fictitiously.   Any resemblance to actual persons, living or dead, events or locales is entirely coincidental. Although, some events are based on the author's first hand experiences.

ISBN: 978-0-615-74024-9

Book design by Dara Ratner Rochlin
Edited by Dara Ratner Rochlin
Cover design by Blue Angel- Mark Snyder
Cover image © 2012 Blue Angel- Mark Snyder

www.pennysnowonline.com

Dedication

I would like to dedicate this book to the English teacher at SRG high school who said I would never amount to anything. Hopefully this will prove you wrong.

Acknowledgements

Thank you to my mum and sister for their support and positive feedback while writing this book. When I had doubts you lifted me back up and made me continue writing.

Thanks to all my friends that are eager to read the book and for being good listeners for months while I talked about it.

A big thank you to Blue Angel- Mark Snyder for an amazing book cover.

Thank you to my editor, Dara Ratner Rochlin, for helping me from day one with this project. Without your skills and creativity my book wouldn't be what it is today. It has been a pleasure working with you. I am looking forward to the next books.

Chapter One

"British Airways flight 321 from London Heathrow to Amsterdam is now boarding. Could all remaining passengers please proceed to Gate Twenty-Six where your plane is ready?"

"Hello, Sir. Welcome on board. Your seat is 3A that's on the left hand side. Please help yourself to a Newspaper and a glass of Champagne."

"Thank you Miss, I will indeed."

As the plane takes off I sip my champagne and have one last look at London, the place I have lived for 39 years. A mixture of feelings overcome me: happy ones and sad ones, but before I can even deliberate or dwell on things the plane is already landing. "Wow that was quick -- only fifty minutes to get to Amsterdam."

I arrive at Schiphol Airport to be greeted by my driver and all-around help, Dedrick. It's hard to pronounce so I will just call him Derrick.

"Goedemorgen Michael. Hoe gaat het?"

"Hey Derrick, I speak English."

"Oh I'm sorry I thought you spoke Netherlands. I was asking how you were this morning. Please call me Dick."

"Ok, Dick it is."

"So where are we headed first, the office or your apartment?"

"None of them. I want to go to a Coffeeshop and smoke some weed."

"Well we will go to my friends' place Coffeeshop City Hall. My friend Dennis owns it and he has the best stuff in the whole of Amsterdam, actually, whole of Holland. It's in the Red Light District on Oudezijds Voorburgwal."

Ok, whatever you say, I believe you. Tony warned me about the Dutch language, he said everything is spoken and pronounced with -kagh or –stract. He said the only thing I needed to know was 'Hoe en start en' and I would be fine. God knows what that means.

We arrive at Coffeeshop City Hall and Dick introduces me to Dennis, and Dennis introduces me to this.

MENU
PRE-ROLLED

Hash   ....   € 3,00
Skunk   ....   € 3,00
Jamaican ....   € 3,00
White Melon ....   € 3,00
White Widow ....   € 4,00
Super Silver Haze ....   € 5,00
Blue Berry Pure ....   € 7,00
Super Silver Haze Pure .. €10,00

WEED
Indica

Blue Berry …..1g.....€ 7,50
Chocolate ……. 1g...€ 11,00
White Melon...1g ....€ 7,00

Sativa

S5 Haze.........1g..........€ 13.00
Super Silver Haze…1g...€ 10.00
Amnesia.......1g............ € 8.00
Jamaica............1g......... € 6.00

This is so crazy a menu for weed. I'm like a boy in a sweet shop. This is fantastic! Legal pot. It's hard to get my head around. I'm in a Coffeeshop with a menu of weed in front of me. Argh! Ok, control myself. Right … what do I order?

I look around at all the happy, mellow faces. The atmosphere in here is so relaxing and Zen-like. Bob Marley is playing in the background and the sweetest of smells in the air. Smells I have never experienced. Wow I think I'm stoned.

Still confused on what to order I ask the guy next to me what he thinks would be good for a first timer. He asks me how I want to feel, and explains that a Sativa is more of a high buzz and could be a bit trippy like Alice in Wonderland and an Indica is more of a mellow buzz like having a bottle of wine.

Ok I think I will have to go with the mellow one. And I will go to Wonderland another day. So I order a PRE rolled white melon.

"Hey! Only take a few puffs if it's your first time. It's strong shit."

Boy he was not lying. I had three pulls on the joint, three very big ones I must add, and man, I tell you I feel like I'm Chong from the movie *Cheech and Chong's Up in Smoke*. I feel good …better than good…everyone looks so funny. I wonder if I look funny?

"Sorry, what was your name?"

"You can call me Stone, my friend."

"As in stoned," I said, as I burst out laughing.

I compose myself and shake his hand. "Thanks Stone. This is an amazing buzz. I mean, look at that picture - has a picture ever looked so good? I mean, how pretty is that girl? Imagine having sex with her!"

"You can."

"What do you mean I can? It's a picture! I know I'm a little high but not that high!"

"My friend, I think you are more than a little high. It's an advert for the Red Light District and that girl works in one of the windows."

"You're messing with me right?!"

"Nope. In fact my friend, I will take you to her window right now if you like."

Jesus! I have only ever slept with one woman in my life. Could I do it? Could I actually sleep with someone other than Kelly?

Well, I suppose sleeping with a hooker is no big deal, right? Shit! Did I just think that? *Sex with a hooker? Not out of the question? Absolutely not!* A hooker. Mind you, I have heard a lot of great stories from my mates in the pub. Even Tony told me hookers are the safest and most pleasurable things to do. In fact, it is a **must** on the list.

Tony also told me that there is no drama with these girls. One: you're paying them; two: they don't kiss; three: they don't get emotional as all they want is the money so they're not in it to fall in love; four: they always use condoms so no diseases. And, five Kelly and me are on a break so why not.

"Mister Stone I would very much like to take you up on your offer. Please lead the way to this beautiful woman."

"No problem, I can do that. I just need to tell you how things work with the girls. Most girls who work the Red Light windows charge €50 per service, so a blow job is one service, a blow job with sex is two services, a blow job, sex and come on the tits is three services; you get me?"

"Yep I do. I totally get you Mister Stone." That's great! A sex menu. God dammit I love Amsterdam.

We leave the Coffeeshop and walk down a little cobbled street, very quaint and quiet. We walk over a bridge and nothing I have ever seen before appears before me - a whole row of red lights and girls standing literally in windows, an amazing display of beautiful women. We walk past 12 windows before we get to the picture.

"Stone, Stone I can't do it!"

"Yes you can. Have a few more hits on your joint, it will take the edge off."

Ok so I take five big hits this time. Instantly stoned but loving every minute and walk in.

Chapter Two

The girl opens the door and welcomes me in with a very cheeky smile, shuts the curtains, then tells me to sit on the bed and asks me if I would like to see the menu.

"Excuse me? What menu?"

"I don't need to see another bloody weed menu," I mutter under my breath.

"My service menu, don't you know?" She then spells out the words S-E-X M-E-N-U.

"Oh I see, well what would you recommend?" I think I'm really stoned. I'm having a conversation about sex menus just like I'm in a restaurant asking the waitress what the best dish of the day is.

"I can tell you have never been to a place like this, right?"

"Yeah you could say that."

"Have you ever been with a girl before?"

"Yes, once or twice actually… **NO** you're right, this is my first time."

"Ok well then Mister…?"

"Oh Michael, Mikey, Mike's fine though. My mates call me Mike."

"Ok Mike, so why don't you let me choose for you. Let's get you naked."

"Ok but I'm leaving on my socks, keeping it British style."

"Whatever you say, Mikey, fine by me. So lie down and relax, I don't bite. *Well… not yet.*"

I cannot believe I am here. I cannot believe I'm looking at one of the prettiest girls I have ever seen; surely it's a dream. I tell you what it is – it's fantastic, more than fantastic. I'm high as a kite on a spliff, butt-naked apart from the socks with a girl that looks like a really young Pamela Anderson. The weirdest thing is if she were brunette she would look like Raquel Welch, or maybe that's just her mannerism and voice. Anyways, she's bloody gorgeous and my dick is hard.

"Ok Mike. I can see you're a little nervous, so I'm going to take it easy on you. Just relax."

She takes off her tight black dress to reveal an amazing body that is covered up by a red bra and red knickers. She takes her knickers off erotically throwing them on me. Next the bra comes off. She gets what I think is baby oil and rubs it very sensually into her pert, big breasts. I think, "Wow! They look amazing. Exactly like you see in the magazines."

She starts rubbing her breasts on my cock, wanking me with her tits then she rubs her tits all over my body, and then she starts sucking on my cock. You cannot imagine how I am feeling right now as I can't explain it in words.

"So am I sucking you the way you like it?" she asks, her big blue eyes staring straight at me.

Gosh you're so damn sexy, I think.

She is in between my legs, her left hand gently moving, slowly massaging up and down on my cock as her right hand clenches the top of my helmet. Then she spits on it and puts her tongue all around. She takes my cock in her mouth up and down just on top, still wanking with the left, after each stroke her mouth goes deeper until she has it all in her mouth. I'm looking down at her and can't help but to push my hands on her head so she can go a little deeper. She looks up at me with her eyes watering, gags on my cock, and then slaps it around her face.

"Oh you're so juicy and hard. I'm going to suck and suck until your cock wants to burst then I'm going to sit on it. Would you like that?"

"Yeah," I whisper.

"Oh that's it! I can feel your cock getting harder. You want my tight, wet pussy to sit on you now?"

And with those words, Bloody Hell I've come.

"OMG! I'm so sorry I didn't mean…"

"Shush, it's ok. You have enjoyed yourself, as have I. I would of liked to have experienced you inside of me, but next time. So how was your first lady of the night experience?"

I have no words apart from ream, which means amazing.

"I got to say though, I feel so stupid. I can't believe I came on a blow job! But it's a compliment to you."

"It's ok," and she laughs.

There is a moments silence then she gets off me, wipes herself with a baby wipe and says, "Ok time is up".

"Of course," I say.

With the weed wearing off and still in disbelief, I start getting dressed.

"Thank you," I say. "Would it be rude to ask your name?"

With a sexy, soft voice she replies, "Penny Snow, don't you know?"

She continues, "I like you Mike. Will you come see me tomorrow? I have to get dressed now but please stop by tomorrow."

I am confused and not sure what to say. Why does she want me to stop by? Argh, am I *that* stupid? Money of course!

This woman has blown more than my cock she has blown my mind. She is fascinating and so captivating.

Without thinking I blurt out, "Penny, give me your number. In fact, I think I would want to see you more than just tomorrow."

What am I thinking? I'm out of control. Do I mean it? All I know is Penny Snow, blonde, 32dd, 24 waist, amazing legs and a perfect bum has won me over.

"Well actually Mike, I'm not working until late tomorrow. I am doing the 10:30 pm shift so maybe I can come to your hotel?"

"Oh no, I'm not in a hotel. I have just moved here. My place is on the Keizersgracht opposite that big Japanese building that's all lit up."

"Yes I know it well. You mean the Okura."

"Yes, that's right. 143A."

"Ok, well I look forward to it."

"Until tomorrow Ms. Snow." I go to shake her hand, and she gives me a kiss on the cheek.

"Seven pm, I'll pick you up from here."

"Sounds good."

My first day in the office and I meet all the staff. Some are clever some are ok. The majority of them are a bunch of gossips. Two of them are definitely cocky little shits that could do with their heads being banged together.

My assistant, a lovely piece of crumpet, is Amelia, but she is not my type. Nice to look at, well her arse is, but her nose is a little too big; but she's a good girl and clever.

I'm sitting at my desk but I can't concentrate. Normally football is the only thing that takes me away from work, but today it's Penny Snow.
I'm getting a boner thinking of her lushest lips around my cock. Sod it!

"Amelia, I'm afraid I have to leave.   I'm so sorry! My first day and all that, but I have heard great things about you and 100 percent believe you can take control of things until I get back."

"Why yes Mister Taylor, without a doubt you can rely on me."

"Righty ho then off I go. On the blower if you need me, that's slang for phone Amelia."

"Oh yes of course."

I go back to my apartment and all I can think of is Penny. What champagne should I buy? Should I get candles? Should I cook? What the Hell! I need help! I lie down on my bed and have to have a quick wank.   I want to last longer this time with her.   I actually want to feel her wet pussy on my cock.
I come hard thinking of her Snow White blonde hair, big blue eyes, and her tits. Then before I know it, I'm out for the count.

Buzz buzz. WTF is that? It's my apartment door.   Blimey that's loud! Who the hell could it be?

I open the door. Standing in just a black corset with French knickers, stockings, suspenders and high heels—is Penny Snow.

"Gosh Penny... Shit Penny… What time is it? Didn't I? -- Wasn't I meant to pick you up from the Red Light District at seven?"

"Yes arse hole you were, it's now 8:30. Stone dropped me off."

Before I could even mutter a word she pushes me back into the hallway and starts kissing me passionately. I feel her hand grab my cock she's rubbing my balls through my boxers. My dick gets hard, harder than I've ever felt it. I pick her up and put her onto the kitchen counter, undoing her suspended belt, pull her lacey French see-through knickers down. Opening her legs wide, really wide I start eating her pussy.

Shit! This is something I have not done for years. Am I doing it right? I start off slow on her clitoris, up and down, side-to-side. I also try and do the letter A, she's getting wetter and moaning so I must be doing something right. I put one finger inside her as I'm still licking her clit. It feels very silky soft, wet and tight. She moans louder then tells me to put two fingers inside her, I do and she lets out a scream.

"Shit, I'm sorry have I hurt you?"

"No, you motherfucker I just came. Now fuck me, fuck me hard."

I shove my cock deep inside her. Shit, without a condom. Well it's too late now. She was right her pussy is nice and tight. My cock is throbbing right now. I'm fucking her hard, holding on to her tits.

"I feel like I'm going to come," I say.

"Oh no," she says. "Bend me over."

"What?"

"Turn me around I want you to fuck me from behind."

Wow. Again something I have not done in a very long time. I turn her around and bend her over. The countertop is a little too high so we go down to the floor. I pull her arse cheeks nice and wide, insert my cock into her pussy. Being a little naughty I rub her bum hole and she doesn't seem to mind. Wow, the deepness I go is immense. She's groaning and asking me to go deeper, telling me to fuck her really hard, and then she tells me to stop. She wants me to eat her pussy again.

"I'm going to come in your mouth," she says. With that, she gushes in my mouth a big long squirt of pussy come fills my mouth. Wow, I only heard stories about that. She then sucks me off until I come. My come also fills her mouth. She dribbles it out and rubs it all into her boobs as if it were the baby oil. We both then lay on the floor with our hearts still beating fast. Finally we catch our breath, Penny gets up and asks if she can have a bath. In fact she insists we both share a bath.

In the bath there's an awkward silence. I don't really know what to say to her. Penny just looks at me then asks if I would wash her back. She ties her hair up, turns her back and sits in between my legs. I lather the soap and start washing her. Gosh her body is so young and silky, it feels amazing. I can't get my head around the fact that she is a hooker working in the Red Light District of Amsterdam.

"Penny can I ask you something personal?"

"Yes Mike."

"You seem very educated and well-spoken. You're obviously from a good family."

She sighs and says, "Yes, yes, yes, you are correct. Why the Red Light is your next question. Well it's something I don't want to talk about, well not right now. I can't. Besides my story is for another time.

I will tell you this though I'm rebelling. I love sex. I love the thrill of working in the window.

And I like fucking you.

Anyway let's not talk about me. What about you? Why are you in Amsterdam and why would a decent guy with obviously money go and fuck a hooker from the Red Light District?"

"Good question, Penny. I'm still wondering why myself. Well, actually I know why, I was off my face, and I'm so glad I was. Everything happens for a reason, Pen, don't you think?"

"I suppose."

"Shit! What time do you think it is? I have to go! I have to be back in the shop."

"Shop?"

"The window."

"Why don't you take the night off and stay here?"

"I can't."

"Look if it's about money, I've got you covered."

"No…no, it's not the money. You see, I sort of have a pimp."

"A what?!"

"Well, not a pimp, more of a bodyguard. I also have to pay rent to rent the window whether I work or not."

"So what does your bodyguard do?"

"He stops pimps from coming up to me and makes sure the right type of guys come in. So if I don't work, he doesn't make money. I know right now I'm his only job."

"Ok look Ms. Snow, let's put our cards on the table. You want money; I want pussy, that's how it works right?   I like you a hell of a lot and I know you got your own shit going on, but what about if I pay the window rent and pay your pimp guy and you take two weeks off? Think of it as a holiday and you can help me get settled into Amsterdam life. Of course I will pay you for your time. Yes, sounds kosher."

"What's kosher?"

"Good, sounds good."

"Ok kosher. Yes we have a deal.   Only thing you pay are my window rent and you pay my bodyguard. As for me, I'm free. We are going to have so much fun!   I'm going to take you on a sexual journey that will blow your mind."

"Fuck me! You've already blown me. You mean there is more?"

"Yes sir. Plenty more."

Shit have I just died and gone to heaven again? This was not at all what I was expecting. How the hell does she know that I have been sexually deprived for years and this is what I need in my life -- sex. I don't know what she means by a sexual journey but I'm up for it. I'm up for every sexual life experience Penny Snow throws my way.

How strange is it - I come to Amsterdam on a job transfer that I must say is a walk in the park, and before I know it I'm having sex with some beauty of a woman.

Although since meeting her I'm losing myself. I'm not the same Mikey Taylor I was two days ago. I'm becoming more of a submissive passive doormat. That's right, I should wear a sticker on my forehead that says walk all over me. Why do men go weak at the knees when pussy is around? Why can't I be my loud, cocky self? Why have I become a bloody puppy dog? It's not right, I tell you, a man should be

18

a man, but I just can't help it. Sex is power. This woman has power over me. Funny isn't it when you think about it. All day long and for the last how many years, I've had the power. I did read in some paper, fuck knows if it's true, but many powerful people are sexually submissive as it's a tension release, letting go. Being something you're not in your everyday life, an escapism. I can't actually remember the actual quote so that's just my interpretation of what I read.

And I've heard all sorts of crazy shit, all sorts of perverted sex stories that involve whips and chains and gimp masks, even butt plugs, but don't worry, I'm not going down that road. That's a completely different level indeed.

Now ladies and gentlemen, it's time for the not so fun part of the book. This is where I have to tell you how I ended up here fucking Penny Snow in the Red Light District of Amsterdam.

It's only seven pages long so you have two choices: skip the next seven pages or carry on reading the fun stuff. But why would you do that? In fact, do not skip otherwise you won't understand what the hell is going on and how debauchery came into my life.

Chapter Three

6:00 am

No…is it really that time? It feels like I only went to sleep an hour ago. Well, at least it's Friday. Thank fuck it's Friday. Wait for it ... any minute now … *'Beep Beep Good Morning this is your wake a call'.* You don't say stupid clock. My wife is still asleep, no surprise there. She insisted on spending £50 on an all singing, dancing, fancy alarm clock, which I knew would be a waste of time; needless to say a waste of £50 and guess what, I was right. It is shit -- who needs an alarm clock that says "good morning, good morning". No, it is not a good morning! When is it ever a good morning?

We all have iPhones these days. What's wrong with the Piano Riff tone, the Xylophone tone, or what about the Bloody Alarm tone? I roll over like I do every morning to give my wife a kiss and every morning she rolls away and buries her head under the covers.

"Morning to you too," I mutter. Mornings are not easy in my house. In fact nothing is easy in my house any more. You can't even take a peaceful shit without the door being nearly taken of its hinges, so these days the morning shit is left for the office. And forget about any type of sexual activity. Not even a wank. No chance. In fact the only thing my dick is used for is pissing out of.

It's a cold morning today, very dark outside and cold air in the room. Yes autumn has definitely set in. I remember in the early days before me and Kelly had three kids, before I got a six-figure salary, before we grew up. How much we liked autumn, the smell of the trees and the colours of the leaves.   Back then we lived in a tiny little studio flat in London Camden Town. Famous for its punk rock and the Camden Lock Market that sells those shitty little hippy trinkets and a lot of that horrible smelling patchouli oil.

Our studio was tiny, but held a lot of good memories.   Everything was in one room. The bed was literally three feet from the cooker and the fridge was used as a TV stand, cosmetic table and make up stand for Kelly's Glamour Bits. Imagine Sid and Nancy that was we, apart from the drugs and killing obviously.   I just mean as in the accommodation.

As for the shower and shitter you had to share that with the next studio flat, so you can imagine how the whole toilet and shower thing was a ghastly, nasty experience.

If I remember rightly the flat next door had about eight people living in it. I think illegal immigrants or fucked up students. Some say it was a whorehouse. Come to think of it, that explains all the comings and goings.

Me and Kelly used to spend days under the covers making love, watching daytime shitty TV like Jerry Springer while eating tubs of ice cream and left over pizza that was two days old and still in the box. What ever happened to those days?

"Don't you dare! I need to use the shower first! Open the door now! Dad! Dad!"

Jesus Christ what the hell is going on? I jump out of bed put my robe on and sort out World War 2 like I do every morning. Teenage daughters Gemma, 14 and Rachel, 16, once sweet little girls, now living nightmares who think they're the only ones on this planet.

Considering we have two showers in the house it makes no sense at all to why every morning I go through the same ritual. The shower room that separates the girls' bedrooms does run really slow. OK, it trickles but it's still water and the other bathroom is three floors down on the bottom of the house, next to the kitchen. It might be a bit cold down there, but the shower's warm.

Well as usual I'm off to use the basement shower, and yes, I can predict it. Two minutes into enjoying the warmth of hot running water on my back I hear, "Babe, babe, Amber's crying." That's our 13-month old.

"Bloody hell Kelly, I'm having a shower! She's crying because she has a shitty nappy, or maybe she's hungry, or guess what? It is morning and one of us has to get ready for work! But don't worry I will see to it."

Why we had another child, I do not know. Well I can't say that, Amber is such a joy in my life, wants for nothing, loves me unconditionally and giggles all the time at me. At least *one girl* in this house finds me funny. We had Amber in an attempt for a boy. I also think, well, I'm more than sure it was also to try and save our marriage. It's done the opposite - it's driven us more apart. I don't mean Amber, just things have changed.

Kelly, I think, has still got that postnatal depression. She's on medication, Prozac, but takes them willy-nilly. She can go a whole week taking them properly then the next week she misses three doses. No wonder they're not working, and you don't have to be no doctor to figure that out.

"Ok, Amber is fed, dressed and ready for Nursery. The kids are walking to school, and I'm off to work," I said.

"Michael, you know you really need to lay down new grass before the frost sets in. Otherwise the grass won't grow, it will die, and we will not have grass in the garden this summer."

"Ok well call a Gardener."

"And you know, the kitchen work tops need to be oiled, there is a big saucepan stain near the fridge. It looks really horrid."

"Ok well get Tony to come over."

Tony is my best mate who owns his own building, painting and decorating company. Our house is so English; it's Victorian, in fact. Attention to detail, down to every stone on the outside. It is overlooking Hampstead Heath, one of the best areas to live.

When we moved in the inside was a disaster, patterned Aertex walls, green curtains, green kitchen, green carpet, everything green. Not even a nice green, a wishy-washy, snotty green. The house even had a loo in the garden!

Tony ripped the whole house out and started again. Now the house is some modern art deco house. It's not quite finished, hence the dripping shower, but considering the size of the place it's taken Tony longer than anticipated.

Even so, it will take him five minutes to put a coat of oil on the worktops to remove the stain.

"Why can't you just oil it? I don't want to look at it anymore."

"Well don't look at it, and, No I bloody can't Kel; I'm late for work."

Gosh why don't women understand? Well I shouldn't say that as a lot of women do, it is Kelly who does not. Why the hell would I want to lay the grass and oil the worktops? I work all day and all I want to do when I come home is chill, watch my football, have a beer and try and have a nice time with my family.

Some things I can't get my head around. Kelly is not adverse to spending money, I mean lots of money, but yet she won't get a Gardener, it makes no sense at all.   Understanding the psyche of women is something men never get, and believe me I've tried. I've read all those books: *Understand your Wife*, *What your Wife needs Now*, *How to be the Perfect Husband*, and *Spice up your Sex Life*. Maybe there should be a book called, *Not What You Can Do but What Your Partner Can Do For You*, and make it law for all women and men to read. Anyway you name it, I've read it, and I'm still no closer to understanding. One book I found was a good read though. *Men are from Mars Women are from Venus* had a slight insight.

"Kelly I will be home late tonight. I'm watching the game, Man United vs. Chelsea at Man U so no doubt we will win and if Man U wins tonight we are in the champions league come on."

"Oh that's just great, off to the bloody pub again."

"No Kelly. It's not the pub.   It's Man United on the TV in the pub, this moment doesn't happen often. I've supported Man United since I was four, and I've always watched the football in the pub.   So what's the problem?"

"Well like I said, it's the grass."

"For fuck's sake Kelly! Just get the Gardener." Another thing women don't understand is men and their football.

I'm a real simple guy considering my job and the money I have. Football is my thing, always has been since the day my brother took me to my first ever game when I was four. Manchester United vs. Chelsea at Old Trafford, I was wearing a red number 8 shirt five times too big for me, it looked like I was wearing a dress. But what a shirt! I still have it today -- the Name on the shirt -- George Best. God rest his soul. Great footballer! He had one million goals in his career.

"Come on Kelly give me a kiss goodbye, and have a good day. You getting your hair done or going for lunch?"

"No I had it done yesterday."

"Oh, I thought it looked good. Yeah definitely looks different. Great cut."

"Michael I had a wash and blow dry."

"Right, yes, of course you did. Ok off to work I go. See you later." As I give her a kiss on the forehead she pulls that face, that whatever face the teenagers pull. Why does she do that?

So that's what a typical morning is like in the Taylor household. Drama. Chaos. Depression. Basically, it's not a lot of fun.

The problem is I married too young. All my mates told me. My mother warned me, her mother warned her to warn me, and my great Nan warned my Nan to warn my mother.

So with all these warnings, what the Hell happened?

I'll tell you what happened. The story goes my dad left when I was three for some fat horrid hooker and has not been seen since. I like to think he is dead and died of all those nasty diseases he got off the whore. That's karma for leaving my Mum for some fat infected thing.

Being brought up just by my mum with no father meant sex was not discussed. The only sexual thing I ever came across was when I had a little glimpse of my brothers' *Hustler*. He held that magazine so tight; it went with him everywhere, he even slept with it under his pillow. I bet the dirty bastard still has it now in his sock drawer.

Kelly, the first girl I kissed, the first pair of boobs I touched, the first girl I lost my virginity to, at 17 ends up pregnant. Thinking I was doing the right thing, thinking I was a man, I asked her to marry me. Unfortunately, the baby did not live. Kelly miscarried at nine weeks. But I married her anyway.

Chapter Four

I work in the City of London at 30 St Mary Axe Building, also known as the Gherkin, designed by Sir Norman Foster. Not that that's of any relevance, I'm just trying to show off. It's actually a unique building. It's shaped like an egg. I actually think its shaped like a bullet.

If you were an architect designing a building, why would you design an egg? After all, eggs are not hard, they break and smash easily. Not good statements especially to terrorists. Yes, come shoot at my egg and watch me break like Humpty Dumpty. Whereas a bullet is hard, it looks fierce and who the fuck would want to mess with a bullet?

I don't drive to work. Can you imagine trying to get from Hampstead to the city? I don't think so. The one good thing about London is we have well run public Transport. I use the Underground and it takes me twenty or twenty-five minutes from Hampstead all the way to the Cannon Street Station.

I'm in the investment market sector. I have private clients that give me their money, and they trust me to invest their money on the right things. And I always have. The clients have doubled, even tripled their investments and I've made a healthy paycheque.

Funny story of how I got into investing. I didn't go to college, as my mum being a single mum could not afford it. Then there was the whole Kelly incident, so I used to stack shelves at night at the local super market. I used to put my whole weeks' wages on betting on the football and I always won. Betting then came to be a little side thing. Every week I would have about ten of my mates give me their money to bet for them. Their teams would win and I

27

would take a little commission. Only time I lost my money was in the pub one Saturday for the Manchester United vs. Manchester City game. We lost.

Anyways Tony introduced me to Greg Slayer as Tony was doing the interior of Greg's office at the time.

"Oh Mike, meet Greg, he does investments. I've just been telling him about how good you are at making money on the football."

"Yeah right Tone, apart from today."

"Yeah but that's a one-off in how many games?"

"Hi Greg, mate. Sorry bad day for me. Man United is my team."

"No worries, I understand mate.   But seriously come and talk with me. Here is my card, I'm looking to put together a team."

"Cheers mate."

So that Monday I called Greg, had an interview and got the job. I'm now the third highest earner after Greg and Simon and have been here for 15 years.

I just can't concentrate today with the game on my mind. It's a big thing. We are two games away from being champions of all Europe. That's of course if we win tonight.

"Hey Michael, can I have a word?"

"Yes of course Simon, what's up mate?"

"Well I just want to ask you something. I don't suppose you fancy taking the Job in Holland?"

"What, leading the Dutch office? Why Simon? That's a great opportunity no commission just a really good pay packet more than you could ever make on Commission."

"I know, I know, it's just… I'm leaving Sarah. The kids are grown up, off to university and we haven't got on for years. We married far too young but stayed together for the kids. And looking back now, why? All those kids ever saw was arguments -- mum crying, me working late so I never had to go home. People always stay together for the kids, but I'm telling you more kids these days have divorced parents and are happy. In fact my oldest, Missy, was telling me that in her school her friends laughed when they knew her mum and dad were together. Me and Sarah have both had a long chat, we are more like brother and sister now, and whilst we still talk we think it's best.

I have missed out on so much life and so has Sarah. I want to go travel, to see the world; Sarah wants to start her own Holistic Beauty Bar. Plus I want to get laid; I want to have a different chick in my bed every night of the week. You know I'm ashamed to admit it, but I've only ever been with three women."

"That's two more than me," I mutter under my breath.

"I'm going to fuck a woman in each place from all around the world. I'm forty-next month, and life for me, my friend, will start at forty. So, what do you say?"

"Shit Simon, I had no idea things were that bad!"

"Nobody ever does, no one sees what goes on behind closed doors. Life's too short my friend, I want to die happy."

"And you think this will make you happy?"

"Who knows but I gotta give it a go…haven't I?"

"Yes mate you do. Shit the whole Amsterdam thing is in four weeks. I don't know… it's a lot to digest, and right now all I can think of is football."

"Don't panic mate. Let me know Monday and good luck for tonight 'cos you're going to need it."

As he walks out of my office he sings,

> "Flying high up in the sky,
> We'll keep the blue flag flying high,
> From Stamford Bridge to
> Wemb(er)ley,
> We'll keep the blue flag flying high."

Followed by:

> "Super, Super Frank,
> Super, Super Frank,
> Super Frankie Lampard!"

Childish. He is, if you can't guess, a Chelsea fan. What amazes me is how many Chelsea fans are now fans just because unfortunately they are a super team.

So I shout back:

> "Stand up for the champions
> Stand up for the champions
> And you're not singing anymore
> You're not singing any more."

"Kelly, Kelly, Kel, we've bloody gone and done it. We have won. Now all we have left is to beat Barcelona then we are the champions. *The Champions Kel!* You should have seen it. It was so tense, we was down 2-1, then before final whistle we scored.   Meant penalties."

"That's great Mike, but I'm tired I'm off to bed."

"What? No sexy time?"

"Definitely no sexy time."

"Not even a quick one? I will be quick.   All you have to do is lie there. Five seconds, I promise."

"No. Goodnight."

Damn it! You know what? Simon's right. He is doing exactly what I'm thinking. I am unhappy, Kelly's unhappy. I'm taking the job. Amsterdam is only an hour away so I can come home at weekends. I could get a nanny so Amber, Gemma and Rachel can stay. This could be the answer to our marriage. Either it will make us or break us.

I can't believe Kelly agreed without any hesitation.   She felt it was a great idea also. In fact, she said that she needed time away from me and she believed some of her depression was due to the fact that she had fallen out of love with me. *Ouch, that hurt.* Saying that she loves me, but I guess she's not in love with me anymore.

So we spent the next three weeks preparing the children and getting Marie the live out nanny to live in so Kelly had help. Kelly even hired a handy come Gardener man to help out around the place.

Something's not quite right with that. The way they act around each other is a little too uncomfortable and suspicious.

But hey, I'm off to Amsterdam.

Chapter Five

It's very black and white with no Grey in my story. The thing with men is we don't have grey areas we are very much black and white. Whilst I feel bad on Kelly, the fact that I'm being naughty, the fact that I'm committing carnal sin is actually quite exciting, wouldn't you agree? It would be no fun without risks, surely that's why men… well I can't speak for you, but for myself. That's why I'm doing it, I'm doing it for the excitement, the risk factor, the 'what if I get caught?' and I won't lie, it's a thrill. Please don't judge a book by its cover, excuse the pun… but hey, me and Kelly are technically separated. Back to the story.

I get a text from Penny on my phone:

<Mike,
A few things:
Strawberries and cream.
Be naked on the bed at 7 pm.
I have a surprise.
Leave the door open and make sure the track (song) "After Dark" is playing from the movie *From Dusk Till Dawn* >

What the hell? This lady is crazy, but I will go with it. The time now is 5 pm so I have enough time to shave my balls. I read that women like a shaven dick as it's cleaner. It also makes it look bigger and I must admit I haven't kept it trim over the years. As I begin my manly hygiene routine, the phone goes. It's Kelly.

"Mike, you ok? We haven't heard from you in four days. The girls want to say hi."

"Ah I'm sorry Kell. You know … moving in to the new office and all that. How you doing babe?"

32

"Yeah I'm fine. Everything's good, believe it or not."

"That's great! Great to hear you on top form. Listen, Kell, I hope it's ok, but do you mind if I wait a couple of weeks before we sort the girls to come over or I fly home? You know, stranger in a strange city and all that."

"No Mike, it's fine, take your time. We aren't going anywhere."

I speak with the girls, a nice but short conversation. To be honest right now they're the last things on my mind. I just want to enjoy my two weeks of freedom, lust, sex, drugs; my teenage years again.

"Ok touch base in a few days." Strange, she sounds ok.

Anyways back to the pruning. I put on my best aftershave, Chanel Bleu and get comfy on the bed. This is so strange. What am I doing lying on a bed naked for some chick to come over and suck me off? I get up three or four times, pace the room, lie back down, stand up, then I hear the key in the door, so like a kid I jump into the bed, press play on the CD player just as I hear the door close.

"Hello my sexy boy! I missed you today."

Looking extremely hot wearing red lipstick, a black bob wig and a fishnet body suit with thigh high boots, Penny says, "I'm so sorry baby, but I haven't been honest with you. Penny Snow is a nasty girl. Miss Snow loves to dominate men and be the boss. Miss Snow loves to be in charge."

With that she blindfolds me, and ties my hands and feet. I feel a little uncomfortable.

"I don't like this Penny, it's not my thing."

33

"Oh baby, please trust me. You're going to enjoy every minute I promise."

She starts kissing me passionately. The taste of her lipstick makes my dick hard. Then the next minute, I feel someone sucking my cock.

"Who Penny? What's that?"

"Don't worry, it's my girlfriend, and she is licking your cock."

Blindfolded with two chicks … sweet! The sensation is mind blowing. Penny takes the blindfold off to unveil another beauty. Both of them lick my balls then they share my cock back and forth -- one sucks then the other one, then both at the same time. Then the brunette, Penny's friend, sits on my face smothering me with her pussy. Penny is on top of me, riding my cock so deep, back and forth slow and every now and then bringing up the tempo. I have never had a threesome in my life. Gosh this is out of control!

Penny then orders Jess out of my mouth and tells her to bend over in a doggy style position. Penny unties me and orders me to fuck Jess in the arse.

Wow! I've not done that. "Penny I'm not sure."

"It's fine," she assures me. She starts rubbing Jess' bum, then starts tonguing it making it nice and wet. She then spits on her hand, rubs the saliva all over my cock and helps me to enter the tight arse of Jess.

Whilst I'm fucking Jess, Penny gets the squirty cream, squirts it all over her boobs and then gets the strawberries and starts rubbing her pussy with them. We are now having a three-way fuck -- I'm fucking Jess and Jess is licking the cream off Penny's tits and munching on the strawberries that Penny has put inside her. Within seconds of being inside Jess I come, then Penny pulls me out, sucks me a little more

34

then starts teasing Jess with the strawberry. She puts it in her mouth, and slowly brings it down her body, tickling her nipples until it reaches her pussy. She starts eating away at Jess while playing with herself. Both girls come in unison, which is music to the ears. Jess gets up and leaves without saying a word.

"Wow Penny! That was insane."

"What? A threesome? You're telling me you have not done that?"

"Gosh no. Of course I haven't." I'm not complaining though. What man could complain with two girls in a bed?

"Penny, I don't get it. What's this all about?"

"Why? What are we doing?"

"I know nothing about you and all of a sudden you're my sex guru. What's the catch 'cos this type of shit doesn't happen every day. Come on what's the story?"

"Please Mikey, leave it. I can't tell you, I wish I could. Just take comfort in the fact that I like you; and like yourself, I see an outlet, a sexual defiance, a sexual desire we both need. I promise you when the time is right I will tell you about me, the real Penny Snow." With that we hug each other and fall asleep.

I don't actually give a shit; I just keep pinching myself. Is this a dream? Will I wake up tomorrow and it all be over? So many thoughts and feelings run through my brain, but not for too long, as at the moment my dick is ruling my head, and like I said, it's a two-week holiday. But I cant help thinking, 'what's the catch? Why me?' Only Penny can answer that, and she ain't ready.

I wake up at three in the morning thinking about football for some reason. Exactly three weeks until the premiere league football starts again. Chelsea's first game will be away so I have time for fun, then football. At some point I do have to make it in to the office, maybe I will go in tomorrow. Who knows what tomorrow will bring. I drift back to sleep.

I wake up to Penny sucking my cock.

"Morning honey this is your wake up call."

Finally a clock with benefits! A clock that actually works, a clock that was worth buying.

"Morning treacle. Did anyone ever tell you you are the best cock sucker in the world?"

"Shut up and come in my mouth."

"Yes ma'am." It takes me a long time this morning to come, and my dick is a little sore from all that fucking last night, but Penny doesn't mind. She is patient and keeps sucking until I explode in her mouth and she swallows it then tries to kiss me, the kinky bitch.

"Thank you. What a nice way to wake up."

"You're welcome, and what a crazy night last night."

"How do you know Jess?"

"I met her at a swinging club."

"A what?"

"A swinging club. Don't tell me you have never experienced that either?"

"Well no … do I look like the guy that regularly swings?"

"Gosh Mike, you have a lot of things to catch up on. A lot of sexual experiences you need to experience."

"You don't bloody say. So tell me what happens in these swinging clubs?"

"Nope."

"What do you mean, 'nope'?"

"It will spoil it. I'm going to take you to one."

Ok, now you know I'm living the dream. So far I've had the most amazing sex by a sex goddess, I have had a threesome and now she wants to take me to a swinging club, whatever that is. I tell you I have never felt so lucky. I'm having a ball.

"Penny, can I ask you something?"

"Gosh, what's with all the questions?"

"I don't know, I'm just curious. I thought girls like you don't kiss."

"What? Whoever said that? It's so funny, you hear all these stories and films that say, 'no kissing, no this, no that'. I do what I want. There are no rules and besides, *rules are for breaking*, don't you agree?"

"I sure do. Give us a snog."

"Snog," as she giggles.

"Yeah a snog, you know, a passionate kiss."

We both start laughing then kissing passionately.

"Penny Snow, is that your real name?"

"Well what do you think?"

"I don't know, you did say there are no rules."

"Well actually, Penelope is my real name, but Snow is not."

"Nice, I like it, Ms. Penelope."

"I'm glad you approve, sir."

"So what's on the agenda today, Mister… ?"

"Mister Taylor."

"Oh cute."

"I thought breakfast, then I do have to go into the office. It's been three days since I have been there and I can't really make any more excuses. I would love to go out to dinner tonight, you pick the place."

"Ok I will indeed."

"Ok my sugar tits, I must get up."

"What was that you called me?"

"Sugar tits."

"What the heck is a 'sugar tits'?"

"Sugar tits is an expression, it's an endearing word. Is that ok? It's actually from one of my favorite all time series *Gavin and Stacey* we will have to watch it sometime."

"Ok. Sugar tits I am."

Chapter Six

"Mister Taylor?"

"Yes, Amelia?"

"Mister Greg has been calling frantically. You must return his calls at once."

"Thanks Amelia, I will."

"Hi Greg. It's me."

"Mike! Bloody hell, Mikey, where have you been?"

"Oh, it's a long story, but I'm here now. What's up?"

"What's up?! The Chinese twins are back. Got four times the amount of money and will only deal with you and Simon. I figured we could put half the money on something Simon's got working on here."

"Hang on a minute. I thought Simon had left and has gone travelling?"

"News to me. No, he is here and has never been happier."

"Oh ok. Never mind. So what do you want me to do on this end?"

"Well did you get the literature on the gold deal?"

"I'll ask Amelia."

"Well read it. I really think that's a winner but I will leave it up to you on what to decide. Just liaise with Simon. How are things going over there? Are you settled in ok? How are Kelly and the girls doing without you?"

"Yeah, yeah, everything is fine; in fact more than fine."

"Ok mate. Well I will touch base in a few days."

"Ok Greg, mate, speak soon."

"Hello Sam. It's Mike."

"Hi Mike. How are you? It's good to hear your voice."

"Thanks, Samantha. You sound great too. Is Simon there?"

"Argh, you just missed him, he has gone for lunch, I'm afraid."

"Ok I will call him on his mobile."

"I'm afraid he has left it here."

"Ok tell him to call me as soon as he gets back from lunch."

"Will do Mike."

"Hello, Kell, it's me, Mikey."

"Oh hi! I wasn't expecting you to call. Everything alright?"

"Yeah just seeing if you're doing ok."

"I'm fine. In fact it's not a good time to talk. I'm having lunch."

"Oh nice. With who?"

"Oh nobody you know."

"Is that a mans voice I hear?"

"It's only the waiter."

"OK."

"I'll call you later Mike, I've got to order."

"Ok, bye then." Hmm… Strange. That was definitely a mans voice, and the weirdest thing… I actually recognize it.

"Amelia, can you please get me the file Greg sent?"

"Of course Mister Taylor."

"And for fuck sake, call me Mike or Michael."

"Ok Mister…I mean Mike. Oh by the way your work experience girl from the local school is here."

"Work experience? You're joking, right? … Nope? Ok, well show her in."

And in walks a tall, sexy brunette with glasses wearing a tight pencil skirt, a shirt with two buttons undone that reveal her breasts, fishnet tights and black shiny high heels.

I thought, there's no way she's in high school. Fuck me! They didn't look like that back in my day.

She shuts the door, pulls down the blinds, drops all my paperwork over the floor then spills her drink over it.

"For Christ sake! You stupid girl! Do you know what you have just dropped?" I jump out of my seat to save the paperwork.

"No, why don't you tell me," she says.

"Hang on a minute… I know you, don't I? It's you Penny! Bloody hell! Give a man a heart attack. What are you doing here, you crazy woman?"

"Well I figured I could be your naughty intern, and now I have just ruined all your paperwork. How will you punish me?"

"I will show you how. Come here."

I throw all the things off my desk, push Penny over the desk, undo my zip, my cock is already hard. I pull up her skirt, rip her pants, and fuck her in the bum hard.

"That's your punishment."

Shit! What's come over me? This isn't me, but I can't stop myself. I push her face down onto the desk and fuck her really hard and fill her bum up with my cum. Then I do my zip up whilst she's still spread-eagled on the bench.

"Now get off my fucking desk and let me get back to work."

"Wow! Talk about role-play. Where did that come from?"

"I don't know Pen, I'm sorry. Was I too rough?"

"No I liked it. In fact, it was not rough enough."

"I'm so sorry to be so short, I have work to do. See you later?"

"Yes, for dinner."

"Great! What are we eating?"

"Pussy."

And with that, she walks out.

Chapter Seven

I finish work and arrive back at my apartment. Penny is not there, just a note saying, 'Meet me at Club Paradise, Schaafstraat 26.'

Ok sounds good. I wonder what music they play? I haven't been to a club in years. The last club I went to must of been when I was 21 or even younger with old school house music back in those days. I loved the song 'Move your Body (Higher)' by the Xpansions. What a tune! I had a few good moves, I tell you. Oh yes I was quite the little mover and shaker. I wouldn't have a clue now.

Shit! What shall I wear? I can't exactly wear a suit. I will have to just wear my jeans and a t-shirt that will be all right. Penny has definitely got me reliving my youth, or should I say making up for all those lost years -- I'm quite excited.

"Dick, can you drive me to Club Paradise please, I'm off dancing." Dick laughs at me.

"Why are you laughing? What? Think I've lost it? Too old, is that it?"

"No that's not it you will soon see."

"…Whatever."

"Here you go. This is it. Do you want me to wait?"

"No, not at all. We will get a cab."

"A what?"

"A taxi back."

"OK, well, have fun."

As I walk into the club there is a very pretty girl behind a till. "Hello, welcome to Club Paradise. Been here before?"

"No I haven't. I'm actually meeting my girlfriend, she is already in there."

"Ok no problem. Ladies are free and it's 75 euros for you."

"Jesus! 75 euros for a dance club -- that's a lot of money!"

"Yes, but it's worth it. Also you get free nibbles and two complimentary drinks. This is your locker key put all your belongings into it. You can leave your underwear on, that's it."

"Excuse me? Underwear? What type of club is this?"

"It's a swingers club."

"A… what?"

"A sex club."

"A… what?"

"A club where men and women have sex with each other. In fact it's greedy girl night tonight which means the..."

"Stop. No need to explain, I can imagine." Holy shit what has Penny done now? A swinging club? I couldn't possibly look at another mans dick. I couldn't possibly fuck in front of people and I couldn't possibly do this shit.

Shit what should I do? Ok let's think for a minute. Penny is in there. Oh My God! Penny is in there! Ok, calm down. Penny did say she was going to take me on a sexual journey that no man has ever gone before. So fuck it let's do it. Yep let's do it. Let's swing. Jesus! Am I really going to do it!

I take a deep breath, walk down the black corridor and immediately see the locker room. I go inside and there are two couples getting undressed. I nod and smile at them, open my locker and start getting undressed. I wonder if I can leave my socks on. For some reason, I got a thing about me socks. Oh fuck it! There's a first time for everything. I take everything off apart from my boxers.

I turn around and the other two couples are also undressed. The men to their underpants and the one lady, tiny body Filipino-looking, wearing a sexy lacy, green all-in-one teddy suit; whilst the blonde, a rather big lady I would say a few extra pounds, has squeezed herself into a PVC cat suit.
I can't help it but I have to close my eyes this is something I really don't want to look at.
I lock up the locker and walk out into the hallway not sure which way to walk, so I just follow a girl in front of me, and end up in a bar area which reminds me of my school disco.

There are a few good looking girls sitting at the bar, I'm pleasantly surprised, especially after what I have just seen in the dressing room. The bar lady asks me what drink I want. I order straight vodka; I'm going to need it. It's quite quiet in here only about 10 couples sitting on tables around the dance floor with a DJ in the corner playing the cheesiest of songs from the '80s and a pole dancer right in the middle of the dance floor doing some pretty nice pole positions. It's a very strange atmosphere, the couples are not talking they're just watching the pole dancer. I finish my drink and order another. Where's Penny? There's no sign of her.

"Hi, how are you?" the girl next to me says.
"You talking to me?"
"Yes I am. You have been here before?"
"No, I haven't actually, it's my first time."
"Oh, a newbie; I love newbies. Do you want to play?"
"Um…I'm not too sure, besides my girlfriend is here," and with that she starts laughing.
"What's so funny?"

"You are. That's why you're here, right? You and your girlfriend to swing with other couples or single girls?"

"Well yeah…I suppose."

"There's no supposing. Come with me." With that she takes me by the hand and we walk back down the black corridor, and go into another room. Nothing is in here apart from what can only be described as a wooden screen with holes in it.

"What the hell is that?"

"Oh, that's the glory hole. Basically you stand behind it and put your dick through the hole and wait. Then random people will just come in and suck you off. It's quite good because you can't see who is sucking you off."

"So… you mean a bloke?"

"Yes, a bloke could."

"Enough of this room, this is definitely not my type of room."

"So let's shower, that's my favorite room." We go to the shower room, and she wasn't lying. I like this room too. It's one big shower and two girls under it washing each other with a lot of soap whilst kissing each other and washing each other's pussies, with five men standing around them wanking their cocks. I obviously don't look at the guys, but I can't help noticing how big some of them are down there. To look at their faces there's no way on earth you would think they were packing something like that.

"Come on get your boxers off, let's join in."

"No, if you don't mind, do you think we could use the other shower?"

"OK."

So we both get under the shower, and the girl whose name I don't even know takes my boxers off, lathers up the soap and heads straight for my balls.

Gosh, it feels good.   She passes me the soap and tells me to wash her tits and course I have to oblige. Her boobs aren't as big as Penny's but nice…Shit! Penny! I got to find Penny! What am I doing with this girl?

"Look, it's awfully nice of you, but I really must find my girlfriend."

"If you must, are you not having fun?"

"I am. In fact, too much fun, but I think I should be experiencing this with her. Why don't you come and play with us? Penny does like a girl."

"Ok, that sounds good.   Let's go find her." We walk out of the shower; I put a towel around me. The girls next to us have a big audience now, and even a few guys have joined in washing the girls.

We walk past another room there's a couple having sex on a swing and the two couples I saw in the dressing room are watching them, so I walk fast past them hoping they don't see me.

Next, we come to this big red room and before I can see anything, I smell sex. I know it's sounds weird but I can actually smell sex -- I can smell baby oil and rubber and sweat. It sounds disgusting, but it's actually an ok smell. Now, I'm intrigued, the vibe in here is very different; it's a little perverted, faster-paced than the other rooms.   So many moans and groans, so much sex everywhere: couples, foursomes, girl on girl, you name it; it's all happening in this room.

Then I see a group of men surrounding a bed: the noises from this bed are very vocal and the men are wanking furiously.   What's going on? I must see! I grab the girls' hand and we find an opening, and what a shock -- it's Penny! Oh My God!   It's Penny!

"Look that's my girlfriend!"

Holy shit! How many men has she got? She has one in her mouth, a guy fucking her from behind,

47

and a girl licking her bum, whilst another guy is touching her tits. I was not expecting this. In fact I'm not at all comfortable watching Penny get laid by another man. I'm actually jealous! Gosh, why am I feeling like this? No, surely I don't have feelings for this girl, do I? Let's put things back to perspective: I'm married, this is fun, so enjoy yourself. I set my feelings aside, and get on the bed next to Penny. "Hey Pen, it's me." She can't reply as her mouth is full, but acknowledges me by rubbing my arm.

I look at the guy who is fucking her, he is really going for it banging her hard. All the voyeurs are loving it: masturbating and couple kissing each other as the build up is getting faster and harder the guy comes, with a come noise I have never heard before. I actually want to laugh, his come noise sounds like a hippo, not that I know what a hippopotamus sound like when it's coming it's just what I imagine. After he is done he pulls out and someone hands him a tissue and plastic bag for his condom.

Then another guy starts rubbing Penny, and starts opening a rubber. Penny stops sucking the guy and tells him to come all over her tits. He does a great gush, and then his girlfriend, or wife, or it could be a complete stranger licks it off Penny's breasts. Penny moves over to me and starts kissing me. "Hello, handsome. Where have you been? Fuck me. I want everybody to watch you fuck me."

"Not here. I have a better place, come with me." I lead Penny away, grab the other girl and start walking back to the shower room.

"Where are we going Mike?"

"To a cool room I found. Oh by the way, this is… I'm sorry what was your name again?"

"My name is Tina."

"Well, this is my girlfriend Penny."

48

"Hi, Penny. You have a good looking boyfriend, I'm looking forward to his cock." We all jump under the rain shower and within minutes we have a couple who ask to join us, so now there are five of us under the shower -- one big fuck fest -- all three girls kiss each other, me and the other gent may I add, do not -- we watch.

Tina then grabs me and we start kissing; she kneels down and blows me, then the mans' wife starts kissing me, and Penny and him start kissing. Before I know it I'm having sex with Tina, and the guy is doing Penny. For the first time I'm actually getting turned on by watching Penny with another guy.

I don't want to finish in Tina though, I want to finish with Penny; so I stop with Tina and pull the guy over and tell him that Tina wants him. I then grab Penny -- I'm so happy she is now in my arms, I kiss her like I have never kissed her before and for the first time since we met I feel a connection that I have not experienced and can't explain.

We lie down on the floor, the hot water still running, and I can't believe I'm using this word, but I feel like we made love…I mean lust. And having an audience of 15 people made me feel good, made me feel like I was the luckiest man in the place, as I definitely got the best girl in the place.

We head back to the bar for a much needed drink. Things are a lot more lively now, people dancing on the dance floor, girls naked dancing around the pole, even the dj has his top off.

"So what do you think? Do you like it?"

"Well I must say Pen, it's not something I would want to come to every week, but yeah it was … it is definitely worth a go. Although it did take me a while to get used to all the men."

"Yeah but they're harmless."

"I know that now, I was just worried that I was going to get bummed."

"No, it's not a gay club. Although the glory hole …"

"Yes, I know all about that and stayed clear. Penny, I know it's only been what…four, well five, days now, but I have genuine feelings for you. I don't know what they are but I have to say, I didn't like you getting fucked by all those men. I felt like they were taking advantage; I felt jealous."

"Listen, Mike. I enjoyed it. It was my first time actually swinging and I loved the fact that I was desirable, that all those men wanted me. Believe me, I was in control. It felt nice having all those men worship me and please me. Surely you felt good with all those women around you, wanting you?"

"I suppose I did. Yeah, thinking about it, I did feel like king of the castle. I actually can't believe I lasted so long. Mind you, I had to think about football a few times."

"And what was with the girlfriend thing, mister?"

"I know… I'm sorry. I hope you weren't offended. I wasn't going to say, 'oh a girl I picked up in the Red Light whilst high as a kite.'"

"Why not? Could've been fun. So what now?"

"I don't actually think I can fuck anymore, what about you?"

"I think I have one more come inside me."

"God dam it, you women are so lucky that you can come and come."

"I'm only joking. I think I've had my fair share, after all it was greedy girl night, and I do believe that I was a greedy girl. Let's dance."

50

So we spent the next two hours drinking vodka shots and dancing. I had so much fun. Sex is so liberating, and I have lived a sheltered life when it comes to sex. Penny amazes me! She is so free with her sexuality, so brave. The things I'm doing now are what most people fantasize about, dream about, but I cannot forget about the real world. I'm a husband, a dad. Shit! What am I going to do? I do love Kelly, but I now have feelings for a girl I hardly know.

Surely I should be doing this with my wife, maybe this journey will make my marriage better. I don't know what to do -- I feel guilty. Kelly would be devastated her world would fall apart. I'm not missing the kids, I'm not missing the chaos, and I do feel guilty for not missing them; maybe I should stop all this nonsense now. Kelly and I have been through so much together, I'm sure we could get through this. I will ring Tony in the morning he will know what to do.

"Mike…Mike…Mikey. Earth to Mike?"

"Yes, Pen?"

"Alright darling? You have been in your own world for the last five minutes. What's up?"

"Oh nothing, Pen, just thinking about work. Do you mind if we head off?"

"Ok Mike, and only because I'm literally fucked will I let you off, although I would of liked to have seen ten women around you, especially the girl in the PVC."

"You're joking, right? I saw her in the changing rooms and there is no way! You're such a tease Ms. Snow. Just you wait, I'll have you over my knee spanking that nice little arse of yours."

"Oh promises, promises."

"Come on, let's get changed."

"I don't have anything."

"What?"

"Yeah, I just came in my coat which is in the cloak room," Penny said.

"Ok, then I'm going to go to the restroom to change and I will meet you back at reception."

"Ok, see you in a bit, Mike."

I go back to the changing room and start getting dressed, and I just can't seem to stop feeling guilty. The time is now one a.m. so that means it's midnight back in the UK.   I wonder if Tony is up.

"Hello Tone. Tone, it's me, Mike."

"Why are you whispering?"

"Because I'm in a club."

"A what?"

"Oh my God, Tone, I'm in a bloody swinging club."

"Jesus let me close the door! Beth's still up. Hang on a minute, let me shout down to her, she's in the living room."

"Beth, I'm just watching the last bit of Game of Thrones, so don't come up if you don't want to know what happens. I'll shout when it's finished. Oh, and Mike's on the phone, I'm just filling him in, he can't get it in Amsterdam."

"Ok give him my love."

"Will do."

He starts talking to me again. "Let me get this straight, you're in a swinging club? Funny, I saw a documentary on TV about swinging clubs last night, not a pretty sight. Oh don't tell me, you did one of those vile loud mouth Jersey Shore types. Gosh you did! What was she like? I bet fake tan, shitty boob job, and a lousy blowjob. You need to come home -- weed smoking, hookers and now Jersey Shore.

When I said you needed to live a little, I didn't mean sticking your dick into everything and everyone."

"No, no, Tone, you got it all wrong mate, it ain't like that. Ok yeah, a little Jersey Shore, but I was with Penny, you know the girl I told you about."

"Oh no you don't, you have not fallen for her! Don't tell me that! You met her in the Red Light District, it's a bit of fun, but you're married. Kelly, remember her? Rachel, Gemma, Amber, remember them too?"

"Yes of course I do -- that's why I'm ringing. Have you seen them?"

"No, but Beth has, and says Kelly is acting strange."

"What do you mean strange?"

"Well, she's wearing makeup and sexy clothes and she's happy. Not the Kelly we know, but that's a good thing right?"

"Yes, I suppose it is. That's good to know, I would hate to think of her still being unhappy."

"Listen mate, you got to stop this Penny thing. You know the woman is possessing you with her sex and you're falling for it. I suggest you bang more than one girl, then you will see its not all cracked up to what it is supposed to be."

"It's to late Tone, I got feelings for her."

"Oh boy, no you don't, your dick has a feeling. Any man's dick would get a feeling when it's being sucked twice a day…"

"Well actually five times a day."

"Yeah, yeah, now you're showing off. Look mate, you got to stop it. Knock it on the head tonight. Tonight do you hear me! Look Beth is going to come up. Call me tomorrow ASAP and make sure you finish it. Pay her double, that's all she's after, dickhead, is your money, you have an arrangement."

"But, Tone, that's the fucked up thing, it ain't about the money. Although it is a bit freaky, I'm experimenting with sex. I've heard of experimenting with drugs but all she wants to do is all different crazy types of sex."

"Well I'm telling you now, dangerous ground. Talk tomorrow."

"Ok mate I will call from the office."

"You took your time."

"Yeah, I forgot what locker."

"Well, taxi is outside. I must say Mike, I'm one tired sugar tits."

"Well let's go to bed."

We get back to the apartment, sit on the couch and the next minute Penny is fast asleep. I stay awake staring at her, as I know what Tone is saying is right. I have a wife and three beautiful children, and I can't throw it all away for A Fortnight of Snow.

Chapter Eight

I wake up in a startle; I too had fallen asleep on the couch. I look at my watch, and it's 6 am. Gosh, I haven't woken up at 6 am since I was in London. I shake Penny. "Penny, hun, we fell asleep on the sofa. Come on let's get you in bed."

"Ok," she yawns. I tuck her into bed and kiss her forehead. "I'll be up in a sec, going to make a cup of tea."

Gosh, I actually miss tea. It's funny the things you miss. The Dutch are not tea drinkers but they do fantastic chocolate milk though. I'm troubled, as I have to tell Penny our arrangement is off, that I am married with kids and explain to her the situation; or I could lie and continue with this double life. But that won't work, that's not me, I'm a family guy and just got sidetracked. Can you blame me? I think by now you can understand my dilemma. Shit, it's only 5 am in the UK, but I got to ring Kelly.

"Hello?"

In a very quiet voice, "Hi Kell, it's me."

"Jesus Mike! It's 5 am."

"I know, I just wanted to hear your voice, and talk to you. Well, I suppose, apologise."

"Apologise for what?"

"I don't know. Not being in touch the last four days. Apologise for letting our marriage go stale. Ask you how you are. I hear you're wearing makeup and sexy clothes. I bet you look great."

"Thanks Mike. Yeah, you know I decided enough was enough of the dressing gown. You know I needed to pull myself together, so that's what I've done and the makeup and clothes actually make me feel good."

"Kelly, I need to tell you something. You know I love you, don't you? Well… Oh God, I don't know how to put this into words."

"Please don't. Mike, listen I'm enjoying our time apart. Have fun! I am. We both need to. Look, you have nothing to be sorry about. You have just moved to a different country. Like you said, in a couple of weeks when you're settled we can make arrangements for the kids then."

"I know that Kell, I'm talking about us."

"Oh Mike, again, just leave it will you? I can't deal with us right now, especially at 5 am."

In the background I hear a man's voice whispering Kelly's name.

"Kelly, who is that?"

"Oh, it's my Dad. He's staying the night. He has a meeting in London tomorrow or should I say today, so it was easier for him to travel from Durham last night."

"Oh great! How is he?"

"Yeah. He is good."

"Let me say hi."

"Mike, no. It's 5 am and I'm half asleep. Speak soon, ok?"

"Ok. Love you."

"Ok. Bye Mike," and the phone hangs up.

Well, that didn't go well, did it? I bottled it, too chicken to tell Kelly. She didn't even say she loved me back. Maybe my marriage is over. Kelly wasn't exactly forthcoming about things was she? So shall I speak with Penny? Shall I tell Penny about Kelly? Yeah, I think I should.

"Penny, sweetheart, I'm sorry to wake you but there is something I have to tell you and I can't sleep another wink without being honest."

"Ok, no problem. Can you give me a second and let me wash my face. Ok mister you have my full attention. What's up?"

"I'm married with three kids." There. I said it.

"And what about it? You don't think I already knew you were married? You're wearing a wedding ring and believe me most men are married."

"So you're not mad?..."

"No, not at all. I wasn't...I'm not expecting anything from you or from us." She takes a deep breath. "Look Mikey, this is an arrangement of sexual debauchery and fun. I don't and didn't think for one minute that we are going anywhere apart from our two weeks of fun."

"Really? So you're fine with it?"

"Of course I am, so get in bed and let's have an early morning wake up call. A little more sleep then you can take me shopping."

"Sounds good. It sounds more than good, it's great."

Chapter Nine

"Wakey wakey, time to go shopping."

"Morning my sugar tits, I'm actually looking forward to this. I could do with a new few bits I haven't been shopping in years.   In fact I could do with a few more clothes that aren't suits."

Penny laughs. "What are you laughing about Ms. Snow? Hey, you're ticklish right there," as I tickle her belly. "Argh, get off me!"

"I won't until you tell me what is so funny."

"Ok, ok stop. I want to go toy shopping."

"Excuse me? Toy shopping? I think you're a bit too old for toys aren't you?"

"Not at all. You're never too old.   Gosh Mike, you are so green. I mean sex toy shopping."

"Oh, ok Penny. Do you know what? You really have to stop being so cryptic. Remember, I am merely a novice at all this, you're the pro, don't forget. I mean Professional."

"Oh shut it Mike green boy Taylor, I know what you mean."

"I'm only joking Pen.   Pro just came out of my mouth. Sometimes I get Tourette's syndrome and at times I do get a stut- stut- stutter."

"Oh stop. You are so silly. And you are right, I am the pro and I don't take offence of my profession.   In fact, I'm very proud and I love what I do so come on, let's go shopping."

"Ok let's go.   Where to first?"

"Well there is only one shop in the whole of Amsterdam that does the most amazing sex toys, it's called the B-1 Erotic Shopping Center, on Reguliersbreestraat. It has the most unusual and vulgar sex toys and there are sex cinemas upstairs, and the best bit is it's not that far from here."

"Do you know what I think will be crazy?"

"What?"

"Let's get a joint and ride to the shop it will be so much fun, don't you think?"

"It actually does sound like a lot of fun, Penny, let's do it. Hang on a minute, we don't have a bike."

"I know. We will just buy one from the junkies in the street they sell them for 5 euros."

"A junkie off the street?"

"Yeah they do it all the time. It's like back at home we have a beach called Venice Beach and guaranteed if your bike gets stolen it will end up down there, but the junkies down there charge more than 5 euros to get your bike back."

We leave my apartment and at the nearest coffeehouse Penny orders a purple haze ready-made joint. We smoke it with a cup of chocolate milk, instantly get stoned and before you know it we are laughing our arses off talking about absolute nonsense. You know when you laugh so hard your stomach hurts and your eyes water that was us. The last time I laughed this hard was when I was at my Auntie Lyn's wedding and her husband was doing his declaration of love. He was being all serious and me and my cousins' found every word funny. I'm sure you've been there. Anyway, well that was we, little school kids chuckling away.

"Right, come on its time to shop."

"One more puff."

"No more puffs. We can have more once our shopping is complete." We leave the coffee shop and within ten minutes, true to her word, a junkie comes up to us and sells us a bike for 5 euros. Well, that's if you can call it a bike. It was so rusty, had a flat tyre and no brakes. It was still rideable, but you had to peddle backwards in order to stop. It did have a basket on the front and of all colours this bike was white. Of all the bikes in Amsterdam we get this one. Well they do say with some things you get what you pay for. It just added to our hysterical laughing.

"So Penny how do you suggest we ride this?"

"Oh it's easy. Put your coat on the back, I will sit sideways and you sit on the seat."

"Ok." Again, another hilarious moment: stoned, riding a bike on the streets of Amsterdam. I never knew how much fun shopping could be.

We arrive at the shop and no word of a lie, it is a shop filled with vibrators and sex aids. Vibrator after vibrator, his and hers, pink ones, red ones, blue ones, black ones, you name it. Every colour, every size, every shape; what the hell? Glass ones. Platinum ones. The list goes on, it's a supermarket for dildos. I tell you something now -- I bet most women have a vibrator. I definitely think it's a must, and a must that every man and wife goes toy shopping. I wish I had with my wife; it is so much fun, such an experience. One I won't forget. In fact, I think you should buy your wife/ girlfriend/ boyfriend a vibrator and put it in their Christmas stocking.

"Hey Mike, come over here. This is the company that I like they're called Fleshlight. Check this out, it's a speed bump butt."

"A what?"

"It's an orifice."

"It looks like a flashlight."

"Exactly, hence the name. But look, when you take the cap off there's a super tight canal and do you not agree it does look like a woman's butt?"

"Yeah, it does. I wonder if it smells like one?" I'm only joking, but Penny says, "Good question.

Let's smell it." It actually smells of plastic. Ha, ha, a plastic butt. "It has beads inside it too, so when you put your cock inside, the beads give you a better sensation."

"Why would a man need one of these?"

"It's a male vibrator. You're not actually going to stick a butt plug up your arse, or are you?"

"Men do do that? Oh there's no way anything's going near my arse even if it is the erogenous zone for men."

"Anyway the Fleshlight is an alternative to jerking off. Not everybody is married or has the luxury of a Penny Snow and I suppose it's a good traveling companion for the businessman. Come on, let's get one for you and you can choose the next toy for me."

"Oh, ok, if we must. As long as you use it on me. I don't want to be wanking on my own."

"Ok I won't leave you alone with her."

"Hey Penny! Check this out; this is the one for you. It's a Hitachi Magic Wand with attachments."

"I have never heard of something more ridiculous in my entire life it sounds like a car."

"Ah, well there you go. I've taught you something for a change. It's got a 5-star review and doesn't need batteries, so unlike Duracell this baby can go all night. Do you want me to read the review?"

"Yes, go on."

"I'm going to use my sexiest voice in hopes that it turns you on, here goes:

The **Hitachi Magic Wand** has come to be known as the 'Cadillac' of personal massagers. If you haven't tried it, you've been deprived for too long. Its strong, consistent vibrations provide sexual stimulation and pleasure that is like no other sex toy, and the soft head makes it great for solo or partner use. With two exciting attachments, The Wonder Wand and the G-Spotter, this package is guaranteed to satisfy.

For over 30 years, the **Hitachi Magic Wand** has set the standard for personal hand-held massagers. Unlike cordless massagers, which use batteries, the **Hitachi Magic Wand's** strong, dual speed motor provides constant power for extended massage sessions.

Material: Medical Grade Vinyl (head soft vinyl)

Vibration: 10 out of 10

Volume: (with attachments) 6 out of 10

Dimensions: 2.6 inches

Requires: NO BATTERIES! Plug-in means no running out of batteries!

"Ha ha, I love it! Yes, let's get that one. Mister Taylor you have impressed me, and your voice … well, feel down below, my knickers are soaking. I'm sure me and Hitachi are going to have a lot of fun together."

"I can't believe this store, it's amazing! I just saw a size enhancer and something called SexVoltz."

"Well the good news for you Mikey, you don't need any enhancement and definitely no penis stimulator."

"You're so sarcastic."

"No, I'm not, I mean it. "

"Well I don't care anyways, now that I have my Fleshlight butt fucker. Penny, I cannot get my head around this store, it's mental. They have come up with everything that one would need for sexual pleasure.   I mean you couldn't imagine this stuff even if you wanted to."

"I told you that you would like it."

"Men always complain about shopping with women, I tell you I'm never complaining again."

She grabs my hand. "Let's go upstairs, let's go into one of the porn booths." We walk upstairs and there is what can only be described as a room full of photo booths. We go to a cashier's desk, change a 10-euro bill for change and get told to go into booth number 4. We put the money in and a library of porn titles come up:

Desperate Slut Wives
Mission: Ass Possible
Porn Wars
50 Sluts of Grey

…So many titles…

"So what catches your eye? What sort of porn are you into?"

"Well to tell you the truth, I haven't watched a lot, I suppose gonzo."

So we go to the gonzo amateur selection, and one film that catches my eye is by a female British director, Ionie Luv Coxxx, by a company called Private.   The film' s title was *Ionie Luv PVC*; the girl on the cover is absolutely gorgeous. We start watching the film, and the booth is small, exactly like the photo booths so Penny is sitting on my lap. I've never watched a porn film before. I didn't tell Penny that. I just remember my brother's Hustler magazine, so that's how I knew about gonzo amateur porn.

It's a really sexy film; my dick gets hard within the first 2 seconds.

"Hello sir, do I feel something?"

"Yes you do, Pen." With that, Penny pulls her knickers down, I unzip my jeans, my cock shoots straight out and Penny sits on it. The girls in the porn movie are so hot that the thrill of fucking to porn in a tiny booth excites me even more. Even writing this now is turning me on; this is one sexual experience you must try. Surprisingly I last for three chapters of the porn film before I come.

Penny pulls her G-string back up, I zip up then we leave the booth and as we leave some guy walks straight in it. "Oh my word, Penny that guy has just gone in there, my come is on the floor!"

"It smells of us, that's why he's gone in there, he's getting off on the fact that we just fucked in there."

"How much change do we have?"

"About 3 euros."

"Excellent, let's have a look at the live peep show." We enter another booth, put our money in and a curtain lifts up. Behind the glass there is a couple on a moving bed fucking. "Penny, look! I can see the guy in the booth across from us. He's wanking."

"I know. Look to the left there is a couple fucking."

"It's awesome Mike."

"Yeah it's pretty cool."

"I wonder how long they have been fucking for?"

"Yeah I wonder too."

"Oh wow, a threesome," and then the shutter shuts. "Shit we need more money, Pen."

"No come on, let's go. Let's go try our new toys."

We get back to the apartment and head straight to the bedroom. "Ok who's first?" Penny asks.

"Well I wouldn't be a gentleman if you didn't go first, so ladies first."

I don't even undress Penny; I just pull her knickers down. I make her suck the vibrator so she gets it nice and wet as we forgot to buy lube. I put the G-spotter attachment on it and place it gently on her clitoris. "It's definitely working Mike. Oh My God I have never experienced something so powerful! Oh My God, this is heaven! Oh shit, I think I'm going to pee myself. Oh my, Oh My God, I love it."

"Shall I turn the speed up, Pen?"

"Oh yes… oh yes… turn it up… Oh My God! I don't want to come yet but oh, oh, I'm going to fucking come. Mike, quick put it inside me."

I quickly take off the attachment and thrust the vibrator inside her. Her pussy is so wet that my hand has even managed to get soiled in her juice.

"Oh yes, yes, yes… I'm coming! Oh My God, I'm coming! Oh Jesus! Mike! God dam it that was so good, you have no idea. I'm shaking. Look at my legs. I'm shaking. My clit is so sensitive, wow! I have never experienced anything like that, and I'm in shock. I've got sex spasms, hot stuff. Come on let get you going."

Penny takes off my trousers. "Lie back babe and close your eyes."
I lie back on the bed and Penny starts sucking me to get me hard. Once I'm hard she puts the Fleshlight butt on my cock, it feels well, weird.

"Pen, it don't feel like the real thing."

"Well just relax and wait a bit, let it warm up. Would it help if I kiss you?"

"Yes it would."

Penny passionately kisses me and I am now turned on. The friction of the beads on my cock feels really nice; the butt actually doesn't lose its tightness, so it hugs around my cock. I'm really getting into it now.

"Oh Penny can you wank it harder?"

"You what?"

"Jerk me harder. Ah, that's it. Yeah, that's it. Arh slow, slow, slow arh, yes that's a good tempo. You were right this feels good. It's a totally different sensation."

"Yep and I have a surprise toy for you. Don't be scared, just enjoy."

Penny starts licking my bum hole. At first I find it strange, I have never had my arse licked before, but with the wanking of my cock and her licking me it feels really nice.

"Ouch! What was that?"

"That's my toy surprise, it's a baby butt plug."

"No way! Get it out Penny."

"Shush…shush…shush. Just relax and enjoy."

"It's hard to enjoy when I've got something stuck up my fucking arse. Ah look, I'm losing my hard on."

"No you're not, it's all in the mind." She starts kissing me again and my hard on comes back. She's wanking me with the toy and fucking my arse with the butt plug: two different sensations, I tell you it does feel good, too good, now I've let go I start to enjoy it. I actually want her to go deeper inside my arse. "Penny oh Penny, I fucking lust you. Don't you stop wanking me. That's it, just do the top of my helmet now, not all the way down… oh yes, oh yes,"

"You ready for me baby? Ready for me?"

"Yes it's coming. It's coming," and I come really hard. "That was great, Pen, but you're a naughty girl getting the butt plug."

"I am but you did enjoy it."

"Yeah I did eventually, once I got my head around it. It was a really strange feeling."

"Which one?"

"Well both, I suppose. You know what, the fleshlight butt was really tight around my cock. At one point I thought it was going to drop off, it was so tight."

"Well you should of seen what it looked liked. It actually looked like the real thing; you could actually see the point of insertion. It looked so real, lifelike, that's why I eased you into it."

"And the arse thing was ok, I don't think I could do that again, but hey Pen this whole day has been so much fun. I don't know why people take sex so seriously. I have to say it, I have had a fantastic day I won't ever forget this ever. It's made me think about sex in a whole new light and you know what Penny, I want to make a porn film. I want to direct one and star in one. Do you think we can do it?"

"Yes for sure. I'm glad you had a good day, I did too and I certainly won't forget it either, toy shopping with Mister Taylor."

Chapter Ten

"Mike, today I want you to see a dominatrix."

"A what? Did I just hear you right? A bloody Dom? I don't think so Pen. You know I have been open to a lot of sexual new and exciting experiences with you and I have had a good time so far, but this is something I'm not into. I know you like to take control and that's fine."

"So why don't you Dom me?"

"I can't, it's not the same. I'm not a dominatrix. A real dominatrix doesn't have sex."

"Well, why the fuck would I want to experience domination if there is no happy ending? Makes no sense at all. That's like me taking the girls into a sweet shop and saying 'have a look around at all the candy but we ain't buying any'. That's fucked in the head -- that's torture."

"I don't think so Mike. You obviously don't understand it."

"No, I bloody don't and nor do I want to."

"I love watching bondage Mikey, it fascinates me. The dungeon. The dark lights. And I love the costumes. The whole idea of giving up control is fascinating."

"Giving up control is a scary thought but it intrigues me," Mike admits.

"Well if it intrigues you, why don't you see a dominatrix and I'll watch?"

"I'm not doing it Penny. I'm sorry, but this is where I put my foot down. *NO!* Penny, I cannot work you out. Please talk to me; please make me understand why and what's all this sex about. I'm starting to think it's not normal, or maybe it is? I'm confused. I have tried a lot of new sexual experiences men only dream of, and may experience a few

68

glimpses over a lifetime or none at all. I've experienced so much and it's *only been a week*. What is in your head? Is it some game you're playing with me? Tell me. If it's about power, then you have it Penny. You have sexual power over me. Ok, I said it. So can we please not talk about any more dungeons."

"Fine."

"Thank you. Not fine."

"I'm seeing the dominatrix, and you can watch, Mike."

"Ok, whatever floats your boat."

"Mike, I'm going to get ready. Open some champagne for me, please."

I walk into the bedroom and Penny no longer looks like Penny. She is wearing no makeup, a white floaty, hippy dress with her hair braided on both sides. She still looks amazing, not like her usual sex goddess self, but very pretty.

"How do I look?"

"Fantastic."

We are off to see Madame Fournier; she is the most experienced in this field and highly recommended. Her place is about a half an hour drive outside of Amsterdam, so we take our champagne and drink it on the way. Penny was quiet in the car.

"Penny, you have nothing to prove. You don't have to do this! Let's turn around."

"No. I want to."

As we pull up, Dick says he will wait right outside the door and if anything untoward happens he will be in there like a shot.

"It's fine Dick, I'm sure I can handle some bitch."

We walk down into a basement to be greeted by an older lady in glasses that introduces herself to us as the secretary.

"So what can I do for you today, boy," she says to me. Penny jumps in and says, "Actually… it's me who wants to see Madame Fournier."

She looks at Penny in disbelief. "You want to see Madame Fournier?"

"Yes. What's wrong with that?"

"Nothing… just we don't get a lot of women, but if that's what you want…" "And him, I want him to watch."

"Well, that's up to Madame Fournier. It's not a freak show for you and your boyfriend to get off on. It's serious business."

"I do realize that Ms. Secretary."

"Ok. Well let me ask her if she is comfortable with him watching. I need you to sign these consent forms that makes Madame Fournier not liable for any bruises, bleeding, injury or death that may occur during your visit."

"Fuck me! Pen, we're going home."

"No, it's fine. It's the normal thing to do."

"Also, could you please tell me what you want from Madame Fournier, as she does not like to waste time? She likes to start right from the beginning."

Penny explains that she wants to be humiliated and hurt. She doesn't mind being tied up and beaten with the cat-o-nine tails or the paddle.

What the hell is Penny talking about, Mike wonders.

The secretary goes away, comes back out and tells us that Madame Fournier will let me watch but she has a condition. I must be naked and tied to the cross. Penny pleads with me, so I agree. The secretary then makes me remove my clothes before we enter the dungeon. She puts them in a plastic bag

70

and leads me in, whilst Penny remains outside the door.

I walk into a room that is in complete darkness. Then very dark, red, low lighting comes on. I see the cross it literally is a cross. Everything is black, even the walls. This feels very strange. Next to the cross is what I can describe as a high bench and there is also some type of swing. On the walls are lots of different types of spanking devices and things I have never seen before, and again furniture I don't recognize and can't even explain. Cages, whips, harnesses. The whole setting is strange, but it is a little exciting, as I have no idea what to expect. My life has been so vanilla and this is very far from vanilla, at the same time it's a little frightening. The secretary asks me to stand against the cross. She then chains my hands and feet to the cross.

"Madame Fournier will not touch such vermin as you so I get the pleasure," she says.

Jesus! I'm actually tied up with chains and shackles. I can't move! Holy shit this is not right. "Excuse me, I'm not liking the fact that I can not move."

"Shut up! Otherwise I will gag you."

I take a gulp and shut up. It's ok, I try to reassure myself. Penny knows what she's doing and I trust her.

The secretary then brings in Penny, and asks Penny does she understand that the safe word is Orange. Everything will stop once the safe word is used. She nods.

"Penny, what's a safe word?" I ask.

"It's just a word you say if things get out of hand then Madame Fournier will stop. You look so funny Mike I wish you could see yourself."

"I got to admit I do feel a right dick head."

71

We both laugh.

The door pushes open. "Who dares to laugh in my dungeon? This is no laughing matter."

A very tall lady enters wearing a leather cat suit and steel spiked high heels with her hair tied high in a ponytail. This hard looking woman, in fact, scary looking woman grabs Penny by the throat and says in a very Dom voice, "Get down on your knees! I command you to get down," without looking at me and strikes her whip on the floor.

She then gets a collar and places it around Penny's neck. Wow that looks tight. I hear Penny make a little choking noise but she seems fine.

"Get on all fours!" she screams whilst pushing Penny hard to the floor with her spiked heel. I could see the force of the kick caught Penny off guard so much so that she hits her face on the floor.

"Up, up, get up idiot," she snarls as she slaps Penny around the head. I'm not liking this but I actually feel helpless, and what do I do I know? It's a game, but still I feel a little uncomfortable. This to me is not sexy.

"Walk, walk!" she demands as she holds the leash of the collar so tight that Penny is gagging and choking. She casually tugs and yanks the leash making Penny stop like a dog would when you tug at the lead.

Then she starts kicking Penny and whips her so hard that Penny actually lets out an 'ow' and then I see a tear drip from her face. All I can think is 'Penny say Orange, say Orange', but she doesn't; she carries on with the torture and humiliation of this woman calling her such vile names, "dirty bitch, weak bitch, idiotic, puny, ugly bitch that needs to know who is the mistress and who is the slave."

She pulls Penny so hard by her hair that a clump of hair actually comes off into Madame Fournier's hand.

She throws Penny into a big dog cage but not before she kicks Penny so hard it knocks the wind out of her. She locks the cage and tells her she "must not bark, she must be happy she is in the cage," and "wag her tail, wag your tail bitch." Penny does and Madame Fournier just laughs at her. "Why you look like a stupid cow wagging your tail." I can see Penny starting to feel a little embarrassed now and her eyes start to water but she keeps wagging her bum as if there were a tail.

Penny then pees in the cage, and the Madame goes absolutely ballistic. "You little dirty, fucking bitch pissing in my cage!" She opens it, grabs Penny's face and pushes it in her own pee. "Drink it!" she shouts, and then she pulls Penny again by the hair out of the cage and rips off her dress, bends her over the bench and starts whipping her. "Cunt," she says, whilst Penny's face is streaming with tears.

I can't take any more of this. "Orange! Orange!" I shout out.

"Orange? Who the fucks are you to call 'Orange'? It's not your word!"

With that she comes over to me, pushes the end of her whip so hard into my throat that I'm now choking. "Don't you ever call Orange again!"

She releases me and tells me to lie down. I do for some reason. She gets her heel and pushes it hard on my chest, really hard so the wind is knocked from me. I start banging my left hand on the floor as I actually feel like I cannot breathe. My natural instinct tells me I got to get this bitch of me, but before I know it, Penny is shouting "Orange, Orange, Please Orange!" Madame Fournier lifts her heel off me, looks at me like I'm literally something she just stood in, looks at Penny and walks out.

In walks the secretary, she hands me the plastic bag with my clothes and puts a sheet over Penny who is still lying over the bench. I quickly get dressed, then go over to Penny.

"Penny? Are you ok?" She doesn't move. I lift her up and she turns into my arms and just cries. "It hurts," she says.

I take off the sheet to look, and Madame Fournier has actually drawn blood. "Jesus Penny! What's wrong with you? What sexual kick did you get out of this?"

Penny sobs harder. "Please don't talk. I don't want to talk. I thought… I just thought," she hiccups through her tears.

"What Penny? Tell me."

"I don't know. I just wanted to feel what it was like to be powerless again, to not be in charge. I suppose I wanted to be punished for what I did to my Dad. I don't know what I wanted. All I know is it hasn't worked. I'm actually not that strong. Mike, I think Madame Fournier broke me she actually broke me! I have never been broken in six years, and this woman has finally done it…"

"Penny, I have no idea what you're talking about."

"Please, let's get to the car and get home."

As we leave all I can hear is the awful chuckle of Madame Fournier "Amateurs," she screams. "I didn't know today was Amateur Day!" She laughs again.

We get into the car, Penny is still sobbing hard. She puts her head on my lap and stays silent all the way home.

"Penelope, we are nearly there."

74

"If you don't mind Mike, I think I would like to stay at my place tonight."

"Why?"

"I just do, ok?"

"But Penny…"

"Please Mike, just drop me home."

"Derrick, please make sure Ms. Snow gets to her door safe and Penny, please call me."

"I will Mike. I will call you in the morning. Night."

Chapter Eleven

I wake up and the first thing I do is ring Penny. There's no answer so I leave a message. "Penny, it's me, Michael. I'm worried about you. Please call me darling. I need to know you're okay. Send me a text or something, please baby. Let me know you're okay. I'm off to the office, you have all the Numbers."

"Morning Amelia."

"Hi Mike. How are you?"

"Yes, I'm good. Thanks Amelia. If somebody called Penny rings please put her through straight away. It's important that I speak with her."

"Ok, no problem. Also, your daughter Rachel rang. She said she couldn't get ahold of you on your mobile, so can you call her as soon as possible?"

"Yes sure. I will call her now."

"Hi darling, it's Daddy."

"Hi Dad. I miss you."

"I miss you too babe. What's wrong? You only call me when you want something."

"Well, I want to go to a club. It is 16-year-old night, and it's from 6 pm to 11 pm, and Mum said 'No'. I think she's being really hypocritical considering you guys met when you were my age and God knows what you got up to. It's not like I'm going to sleep with any boys, drink or take drugs so I don't see what the problem is. I need you to speak with her."

"Well, hun, if Mum says No, it's No. What can I do from here?"

"Can't you at least try and persuade her? Would you let me go?"

"I'm not sure Rachel, I have to think about it.

I'll have a chat with your Mum and see what I can do. Tell me how's things? How's school?"

"School is still the same as it was a week ago, and Mum seems in a good place. She's been going out a lot, and the other night Simon came over and had dinner with us."

"What? Why would Simon come over and have dinner?"

"Oh, because he dropped over some paperwork for you. I don't really know Dad. Anyway, Billy is on the other line, I have to go."

"Ok, well, Love You."

"Yep. You too, Dad."

"Amelia, please get Simon on the phone."

"Hey Simon, it's me Mike. Hey mate, listen Rachel said you stopped by the house the other night. Everything okay?"

"Ah yes, I couldn't get hold of you. You have been MIA. I'm sorry mate, I know the truth, don't worry -- first time in Amsterdam and Coffeeshops and don't tell me, those windows in the Red Light…"

"No, none of that. So what papers?"

"It's just the contracts for the deal. I wasn't sure if you were coming home over the weekend, so I left them with Kelly. But what I'm thinking is I'm going to fly out to the Dam tomorrow then we can go over everything then. I haven't been to Amsterdam for years myself, so we can work and play. I'll get Sam to book me a flight now. I will get to the office for 11is what I'm thinking. Ok mate?"

"Sounds good, see you tomorrow. Oh and Simon? Bring some tea bags would ya? The tea is shite here."

"Will do. Get those Heinekens' ready."

"Mr. Taylor, Mr. Taylor. Penny's on the phone."

"Oi! I have to go. I have to take this important call."

"Hi Penny."

"Hello Mike."

"You ok?"

"Yeah I'm ok, I think."

"I've been so worried…"

"Do you think you can come and meet me?"

"Yes. Sure babe. Where are you?"

"I'm at my place, the shop."

"What are you doing there? You're not working, are you?"

"No, I just came. I don't know… I feel safe here."

"Ok, I'm on my way. I will see you soon."

"Amelia, I have to go. Please do not transfer calls to my mobile. Take messages. Anything important, obviously ring me ASAP also can you get some Heineken beers in? Simon from the London office is coming tomorrow."

"Okay. Got it."

I jump in the car. I do hope Penny's ok. Last night freaked the hell out of me. It's weird, I've known Penny for a week now and the topic of her being a prostitute hasn't even come up. She doesn't even look like one, I don't think. Well, it's not like I would know anyway, and the strangest thing is that it hasn't even crossed my mind either. It's really strange.

"Just drop me here, please Dick. I can walk the rest."

"Ok. Shall I wait?"

"No, I will call when I need picking up."

"Penny…Penny! Jesus, Pen!" I walk in and Pen is hunched up, her knees tucked into her head crying, still wearing the sheet from last night's events.

"Have you been here all night?"

"Yes."

"What's wrong with you? Come on and wash your face. Your mascara is all over it and you look like Marilyn Manson." She smiles.

"That's better. Come on, put some clothes on. Let me go and get you a drink and a sandwich."

"I'm not hungry. I could do with some wine though."

"Ok, you get dressed and I'll be back in a sec with some supplies."

I return to Penny wearing black leggings and a t-shirt, all her makeup off. Gosh, she is really pretty. She looks like a different Penny, but still really pretty. "Here we go darling: fries and mayonnaise, I could not resist and a bottle of red."

Gosh, this place looks different in the day, or maybe it looks different because I'm not stoned. It's surprisingly small and bare, very clean with white tiles on the floor, a single bed, a sink and a full-length mirror on the opposite wall and a shitty little DVD player.

Now this is a reality check. It's not at all glamorous, in fact it's very sad. Oh gosh, to think my Penny gets violated night after night in this place! I can't bear to picture it.

"Penny, what are you doing here? I don't understand why you need to work here. You're much better than a prostitute."

"How dare you! How dare you speak to me like that! You know nothing! Some girls don't have a choice. Some girls are trafficked and are forced to be prostitutes, some as young as 14. Some girls are

79

damaged goods. Some girls are drug addicts and need the money. *And*, some of us, *me included*, are well educated, and don't need the money but love having sex, love the thrill of having sex, being adored, having sexual power over men.

You know what Mike, it's me who has the last laugh. *Me*. I love sex with strangers and I love taking their money. Prostitution is one of the oldest professions in the world. In fact, it even goes back to the Bible. How dare you judge me! How dare you! You weren't put on this earth to judge another human being and so many people do. It's bullshit! If a woman wants to charge men for sex, enjoys having sex, then why should anyone care? Why should it matter to them? Sex should be something enjoyable not something frowned upon. Sex between two, three, four consenting adults is nobody else's business. Yes, not everybody is into swinging and porn movies but don't judge someone else's sex life. More men and women should try their fantasies and not be afraid, and maybe the stigma that comes with sex wouldn't be there."

"Ok Penny, calm down. I'm sorry. I didn't mean to upset you."

She cries, "Please hold me." I hold her tight until she stops crying.

"Let's open the wine. I want to tell you something, but please don't say a word and just listen." She takes a drink from her wineglass, and starts.

"I'm not really a prostitute. I have money, lots of it. I bought this building and upstairs is a safe house. At the moment there are 20 girls living here -- girls that have come from poor countries, they have made their way here to earn money. I can't stop them from working, they choose to. But what I can do is make sure they have a safe environment to work from and make sure they don't have pimps coming to get them and that no harm comes to them.

I also have three ladies that are in drug rehabilitation that have been working the windows for a long time and want to get clean and stop working. My team and I are helping them figure out what their next steps are going to be -- counseling them and getting them clean.

I have also got a few girls that are students and are doing this to pay for their University fees.

Then, there is Jess. She is the girl who just loves sex, she has no bad background, no sad story to tell. She just loves sex and gets a thrill out of being paid, although she is picky as she only lets the good looking ones in."

Penny pauses, and drinks some more wine, before continuing.

"And as for me, this is my cover. I have slept with a few guys, some because I fancied them, and some because it makes my cover look more realistic. The night I met you, Stone called me. I had been moaning to him a couple of days before saying that I was never going to meet a normal guy working in the window. Stone doesn't know any of what I'm telling you, he thinks I am a working girl. So he rang me to say that he had met a lovely English guy in the Coffeeshop and that he thought you would be my type. When I saw you I knew he was right, and like I said, I instantly got a connection with you.

I grew up in a place called Baltimore, Maryland, which is close to Washington DC. We had two houses, one close to the city in Patterson Park and another home out in the country. My Dad is

81

a diplomat, an ambassador, in fact, quite high up. We used to go to such lavish parties and I met lots of interesting people from all around the world. My dad's circle was mainly British. I suppose that's why I have such an affinity for the British language. You couldn't tell I was American, could you?"

"Not at all. Mind you, that does explain your twang," Michael said.

"My mom was a stay-at-home mom looking after me, my brother, and my sister . My brother is now 21, my sister, 24, and I'm 27. We got brought up strict Catholics -- Catholic school, church twice a week, and Sunday School."

"What's Sunday School?"

"Well after church, we would stay in the church. We would clean the pews, we would prepare the leaflets for the next service, and we would pray and learn about God. I wasn't allowed boyfriends and was taught no sex before marriage. I took my religion seriously, but hated it at the same time, as we were freaks. I wasn't allowed to do the things normal girls were doing my age: makeup, boys, school proms. I used to get teased.

There was absolutely no mention of sex. That was a forbidden word. Anything remotely sexual that came on TV my parents would turn it off. We couldn't even go to the movies without our parents consent just in case there was a sex scene in it.

My first boyfriend was at the age of 17. I had to sneak out of the house and pretend I was doing afterschool activities to see him, and then a year later I left to go to college, so that ended. I met Tom after that and was going to marry him when I left college just so I could have sex. I was too scared of what my father would do if I had sex before marriage. I never made my final year in college as I left and fled to Amsterdam. Gosh I miss my sister and brother so much. I wonder what they're doing now? My brother if he is still in college? My sister if she is married?

I was on Spring Break when my friends and I decided we would go to Los Angeles and hang out in Venice Beach. One of my friends' dad had a beach house and we had all turned 21, the legal age for drinking, so we planned to have a big old party full of alcohol. I got a phone call from my sister who at the time was 17 still in high school and living at home."

"Penelope," she said, "you better come home. There have been problems for months. Mom is drinking every night and passing out. She found out that Dad has been having an affair, not with one but two different people and there's more… For the last ten years, Dad has been involved with the mob, gangsters, really bad people, Penelope. He has been using his position to launder money for them, getting them out of trouble and doing dodgy things with the government."

"How do you know all this," I asked.

"Because something was up with my computer and no one was home so I thought I would use Dad's. There was a document that he had forgotten to close; the first line said, 'This is my confession. If anything should ever happen to me, please look after my family.'"

"It was addressed to someone high up in the government, my sister thought. She told me the document had pictures of men, pictures of money, drugs, passwords, names and addresses, and a day-to-day account of every dodgy thing he did.

So I went home immediately and read it for myself. I felt sick to my stomach. All these lies, making me suffer all my life, making me feel like a freak, not having a normal teenage life because of some religion that was forced on us. I just couldn't believe my Dad, who pretended he was holier than anything was a cheating, lying, stealing con man. And as for my mom, it turned out she knew about the other women, and just let it happen again and again. How could she? She too was a hypocrite.

So that night, I decided to leave. I couldn't be around these people any more. My sister begged me, my brother didn't give a shit. Both of them could just turn a blind eye but I couldn't. All those years I could of had sex with Tom, I didn't have to get married.

Anyway I went down into the basement to find a suitcase. I found a big, black one that I hadn't seen before, and it was heavy. I opened it and it was full of hundred dollar bills. I didn't count it, and still haven't. All I know is that it must be millions. This building cost me one million euros, and I have been here for six years spending the money.

I got my passport, went straight to Dulles International Airport in Washington DC, and sat there with no clothes, nothing, just a suitcase of money. I saw the departure board and there was a plane to France so I bought a ticket, and flew to France. Three days later I rang my sister. She told me that Dad nearly got killed because of the missing money, but he managed to sort out the release of one of the biggest drug barons in the world that was doing a life sentence in jail. So somehow, and God knows how, they told my father that the missing money could be payment for his work and that he would forever be indebted and would now have to work for them for free.

Then my sister told me, that even though it was all cool, she felt that men like this don't let this type of thing go that easily. She said out of principle they would probably look for me and for my own safety I should go far away, never ring, never tell anyone where I am, and get a new identity; so that's what I did. My brown hair, brown eyes, and small breasts became blonde hair, blue eyes and big tits. Then one night I was watching *Scarface*, the movie, and I imagined the men my Dad was working with were like that: that they would find me and kill me. It freaked the hell out of me so I walked around Paris all night, plotting where would I be safe where no one would find me. I was thinking a nunnery or maybe go to India to one of those retreats. So many things were running through my head. And I felt scared at one point, I thought well I will just go home.

That was until I met Kitty, a working girl, she was having a cigarette in front of a really pretty building, it turned out that it was the Moulin Rouge. I needed to smoke so I asked if she had a spare cigarette, she did and we got talking. I told her I was a tourist and she asked if I wanted to join her, and I'm so glad I did. We went to a burlesque club, a strip club, I had the best night of my life! I felt like such a rebel and I liked it, then I went back to Kitty's house and she told me stories of all these exciting places she had been to, and stories about her clients. Some of the sex stories sounded fantastic, in fact every story she told me sounded fantastic, and then that night back in my hotel room it came to me. I'm going to Amsterdam. Who would think to look for me there? There's no way in a million years anyone would think I was a prostitute in the Red Light District. So here I am."

"But that doesn't explain last night, Penny."

"Every now and then, I get sad and feel bad for what I did to my family, my mom, brother, sister, even my dad. For all they know, I could be dead so yesterday was one of those moments, and like I said, I felt I needed some punishment. I wanted to be hurt for the hurt I've caused. I know it sounds fucked up Mike."

"Yeah, it does Penny, and what about the sex stuff?"

"Well I decided to use the money, drug money, whatever it is, and do some good with it. I can't explain why the sex thing, and why I'm experimenting; all I know is it makes me feel alive; it makes me feel great. It's exciting, it's living on the edge, it is debauchery since I don't feel like a freak when I'm Penny Snow. I suppose in my subconscious it's a 'fuck you' to my parents as they would have a heart attack if they could see me now. And besides, I'm not getting any younger, so why not."

"Jesus Penny! I don't know what to say. It sounds so unbelievable, it sounds like a movie. Wow."

"Yep and that was the short version. One day I will tell you the full story. And another thing, I know it's only been a week, but Mike I think I'm falling for you too…"

"But yesterday you said…"

She puts her fingers to my mouth and starts kissing me. "Shush, forget yesterday."

"Well you know I've fallen for you." I can't believe I said that back to her! I can't believe it! I'm in real shit now a wife and a girlfriend. Help! Somebody?

"So what now Penny?"

"What do you mean, 'what now'?"

"Well, what should we do?"

"Nothing. We go back to our normal selves, Penny Snow and Mike Taylor and finish our two weeks of sexy time.   Come on, let's go back to your place, get stoned and make love."

"Ok I just need 5 minutes to digest all of this. I have to say I'm a little scared."

"Nothing is going to happen Mike, it's ok. Come on Mike, forget what I told you Mike. Please don't let what I have told you change anything and please let's not ever talk about it again for the rest of the week.   I've been here for six years and I have been fine. This is the second time in those six years I've broken down. I love my life here, I love the work I do with the girls, and I love having sex with you. So come on, let's go.
…And besides, I'm so hungry now."

"Yeah? What are you hungry for?"

"That's a stupid question."

"Why's that?"

"I'm hungry for cock."

Chapter Twelve

I wake up and the clock says it's three am. I can't sleep. Penny is fast asleep, but me, I can't get out of my head what Penny told me, and I also can't get Kelly out of my head. I'm so confused. I'm falling in love with Penny and I do love Kelly, but not in a husband-wife situation. I know I'm not *in* love with her anymore, but nevertheless, I can't have them both. I have to decide what is best for the kids' sake and especially baby Amber. I should sort things out with Kelly, but then on the other hand I want Penny.

Some guys are good at this. One of my mates he has been married for years and has been having an affair as long as he's been married, not me. I couldn't and I wouldn't want my kids to be fucked up because of an affair.

I'm going to have to tell Kelly, it's the right thing to do. I will go to the office early before Simon gets there. I make some chocolate milk then go back to bed.

My alarm wakes me at seven am. "Penny, hun, I have to go into the office. Simon is coming so I'm not sure how the day or evening is going to pan out so I might not get to see you but I will keep in touch, ok?"

Penny says still half asleep, "I hope it goes well for you."

"Thank you." I give her a big kiss then I leave.

"It's cold this morning Dick, don't you think?"

"Yeah it is, but Amsterdam is still a beautiful city any time of the year. It is great when the dams freeze everybody goes ice skating."

88

"Dick, Simon from the other office is coming today."

"Yes, I know. I'm meeting him at the airport. His plane arrives at 8:45."

"Wow that's early. What's the time now?"

"It's 3 minutes to 8."

"Ok, thanks." Shit! I haven't got long to chat with Kelly. I jump out of the car and run up all the stairs.

"Amelia please don't let anyone disturb me. I have an important call to make." I pick up the phone and dial Kelly's number, there's no answer. She has to be up its only 7 in the morning in London.

I ring Rachel's phone. "Rachel, it's Dad. Is Mum there?"

"Yes she is in the shower."

"Ok can you call her, please it's important?"

"Mum, Mum… Dad's on the phone."

"Tell him I will call him back."

"No sweetie, tell her I need to speak to her now. It's important."

"Mum, Dad said it's important."

"Jesus Mike! What's so important that it can't wait till I have finished my shower?"

"Can you go into the bedroom where the kids can not hear you please? I will call you on the home phone."

"Hi Kelly. Look we need to talk. I need to tell you something and you need to be honest with me and I'm going to be honest with you."

"Ah, Amber's crying now Mike. I've got to see to her. Let's talk later."

"Well, can't you ask one of the girls to see to her? Simon will be here soon and I need to talk to him too."

"What do you need to talk to him about?"

"I just do."

"Well I will call you back in five then, ok?"

I sit and watch the clock. Five minutes go and pass; ten minutes go and pass; 30 minutes go and pass; still no phone call from Kelly. I ring her mobile and then the house phone, no reply; I keep ringing and ringing only to get the bloody answer phone message. "Hi, you've reached The Taylors. We can't take your call right now. So please don't hang up and leave a message. Have a good day."

"Kelly you said five minutes it's been 40. Call me back please. If you are there, pick up the phone. It's quite frustrating you know." I put the phone down and in walks Simon.

"You got here quick."

"I sure did. I want to make the most of Amsterdam, so I thought business then pleasure. Nice office, nice building; in fact, sexy secretary have you had a go?"

"Don't be silly, Simon."

"I'm not. If I were in your shoes, I would be all over that."

"Well I'm not you, and I'm not. I'm married, remember?"

"Yeah but you're on a break aren't you? So technically it doesn't matter."

"I suppose not, but she ain't my type. Anyway, let's not talk about Amelia, my secretary. How are things with you? I thought you were leaving the company and going traveling."

"I was but a change of plans. *Love, my friend.* My new bird doesn't fancy it."

"You have a new girlfriend?"

"Yep, I've known her for years. It's only been six months but it's the real deal. I never thought it

90

would be possible to find the woman of my dreams. She is my life long partner."

"Oh good for you mate! I'm happy for you. What's her name? Do I know her?"

"No, not sure you do. Anyway, look, let's get the business done then we can go explore Amsterdam." So we spend the next five hours sorting out the business proposal for the Chinese twins and both agreed we shouldn't split the money we should invest it all on the gold proposal I'm dealing with and I would just give Simon a lesser percentage of the deal.

"So I'm glad we sorted that out. It only took us five hours."

"Why, what's the time?" Simon asks.

"Two. I will get Amelia to email everything over. And now I think it is time we had a well-deserved beer."

"I agree."

"Amelia stocked up. We are loaded with cold cans of Heineken. Isn't it funny how Heineken tastes different here than it does in London?"

"Yeah, it does. I wonder why."

"I thought that too. There's this great little Dutch bar that serves it on tap. We can go there and they also do the best cheese fondue and cold meats."

"That sounds good." We go to the bar, drink a shit load of Heineken and eat a shit load of food. Then Simon wants to go to a Coffeeshop to get stoned so I take him to City Hall.

"Hi Stone, this is a good friend of mine Simon. We also work together. He was supposed to be running the office."

"Oh very good. So, what happened?"

"It's a long story. Anyway what do you recommend for him? He wants to get really high."

"Alice in Wonderland high? As high as a kite high? Then he should smoke Train Wreck."

Simon says okay.

"How's Penny, Mike? I haven't seen her for a while."

"Who's Penny?," Simon asks.

"Ah… Um… she is my um… my um..."

Stone jumps in. "Cleaning lady."

"Yes that's right, she's my cleaning lady! She slipped yesterday and hurt her finger. Nothing serious." I wink at Stone he nods back. "Enjoy boys, I have to go."

Once Stone is gone, Simon says, "Here have a puff on this. This is great shit. It's an instant high. Gosh, the last time I smoked was on my stag night a long time ago."

"No I'm ok. Drinking and smoking doesn't work for me, it's one or the other."

"I'm really high Mikey, this is great! Come on try some. Let's be Train Wrecks together."

"No, honestly I'm fine. I would go easy on it though, it will blow your mind." And I wasn't wrong, within 30 minutes Simon went from all happy to pale faced, his head was spinning, and he was having a whitey. He couldn't even stand up. Shit, this is all I need. I ring Penny.

"Penny, Penny, it's me. Listen, are you still at mine?"

"Yes I am, why?"

"Simon has pulled a whitey."

"What's a whitey?"

"He smoked too much, he is spinning out, not making any sense and not coherent. I'm going to have to bring him back to my place and he can't see you."

"Ok, well I will go to mine. Give him orange juice or hot water with a lot of sugar in it, that normally sorts it out."

"Ok thanks. I will call you in a bit. I'm so sorry Penny."

"No, it's fine."

"Simon. Drink this mate, it will make you feel better."

 He drinks it. "I think I'm going to puke mate." I help him outside and he does puke. He is sick all over the pavement and even his shoes.

"Dick can you come to the Coffeeshop? Simon is stoned and I need help getting him back to my place."

"Ok I will be there in five." We get him back to my apartment; carry him up five flights of narrow stairs. They seem not to have lifts in buildings in Amsterdam for some strange reason, or maybe they just don't in mine. We get him into my bedroom; take his jacket and shoes off. Dick cleans his shoes. I put a bucket by the bed and go into the living room, sit down and digest it all.

The next minute, I hear the Dallas ring tone. Jesus what's that? It keeps ringing. You know the tune, 'da da da da da da da da da da da da da daaaaa da daaaa'. What a hideous ring tone! I can't listen to that, so I go into Simon's jacket pocket, pull out his mobile phone to switch it off and see 6 missed calls from someone called Kelly. Hmm, strange. Why's Kelly calling Simon?

I grab my phone and my battery has died. Ah! That's why she is calling, to get a hold off me. I will call her back from Simon's phone. Then I hear a beep on his phone saying that he has one new voicemail so I listen:

"Hi Simon. It's me Kelly. Please ring me ASAP. Why are you not answering? I think Mike knows everything. I think he knows about us, about the whole Amsterdam set up. Please call me. We need to stick to the same story. I love you and I'm missing you."

No! Did I just hear right? I play the message again. In fact, I play it three times. I can't believe this my wife… and Simon! I'm going to throw up! I run to the kitchen sink, I'm physically sick. No! Not Kelly and Simon! What set up? No, not Penny too! I start crying. I want to go in that room and beat the shit out of him but I don't.

I run outside, grab a cab and go straight to Penny's window.   She's not there; another girl is in the window.   I barge in, grab the girl, "Where's Penny? Where's Penny?" I say, shaking her.

"Stop it! You're hurting me!" the girl says.

The next minute the bodyguard is wrestling me to the floor. "You can't barge in here and touch this lady."

"I need to see Penny."

"Well you can't."

"So tell me where she is as I need to see Penny now. I won't leave until I do. I will cause a scene and you wouldn't want that, would you?"

"Ok calm down. Wait by the bridge and I will get Penny."

I walk over to the bridge and cry.

"Mike, Mikey… what's wrong? What happened?"

"Is it true," I ask her with tears streaming down my face.

"Is what true?"

"You know what Penny. Don't give me this bullshit! I told you yesterday I thought your story was unbelievable." I grab Penny, shake her, and cry, "I

94

loved you! I do love you! For God sake… Why? Why?"

"Mike! Stop it! You're scaring me. I don't know what you're on about, I promise."

"So you're not in it with Simon and Kelly my wife? You're telling me that they didn't hire you to fuck me so they could get away with their seedy affair?"

"What! What are you talking about? No, no, I promise I don't know what you are on about. Look at me. Please Mikey look at me! I love you! I love you! I love you! I would never do anything to hurt you. Come on, calm down. Let's go to City Hall we can talk."

"Can't we just go into yours?"

"No, we can't. It's a safe house, so no men up there. I'm sorry. Why don't we go sit in my car?"

"I can't believe it Penny…"

"You need to calm down and tell me what's happened…"

"Thinking about it I should of known all the pieces to the puzzle are there, Penny. Kelly's been depressed for months. The minute I leave she snaps out of it, wearing makeup and sexy clothes, getting a good looking Gardner to throw me off the scent so if anything I would think it was him. … The lunch the other day with the man's voice. … Oh no! He's been in my bed! That wasn't her Dad that was *him*. …He's eaten at my table with my girls … my children. Gosh they both set me up. He was never taking this job; he was never leaving to travel around the world. Yes he was leaving; he was leaving his wife for my fucking wife! And Kelly? How could she? She has made the last six months for me a living hell. All done on purpose. I see that now. She made life at home so unbearable that I would take the job. I feel sick.

How could she do that to me? The kids? What sort
of woman is she? What sort of guy is he? I'm going
to knock his head off his fucking shoulders!"

"No you're not Mike. Listen to me. I know
you are hurt. I know you are upset, and it is awful
what they have done. I get that. But look at one
positive thing that has come out of this: you met me.
You met *me* Mikey, and we have fallen in love, so we
should be thanking them. Well, I should be thanking
them for putting you into my arms. Mikey. Please
believe me when I say these words: I love you."

I open the door and get out of the car. "Mike,
Michael where are you going? Come back here."

"I'm going for a walk. I need to be with my
own thoughts for a bit."

"Okay. Please don't do anything stupid. I will
wait in the car for you."
I walk around for about an hour deciding what I was
going to do, what I was going to do to the both of
them.

I get back into the car. "Thank you Penny.
You're right, I did meet you and I have fallen in love
with you. This morning I was going to tell Kelly
about you and I was ready either way for Kelly to tell
me to get lost and it was over, or for her to tell me
she would forgive me and we would work things out.

The reason for working things out wasn't
because I'm still in love with Kelly, it was for our
children, but she is the one who has fucked it up not
me. I don't want to put my children through pain,
look how much you are hurting from knowing that
your dad had an affair. I don't want my kids to hate
their mother or hate me so I will speak with Kelly, tell
her I know and that we must tell the kids we are
separating, that way they won't hate her for having an
affair. That's why she didn't want sex with me

96

because she was screwing someone else. What a mug I am.

And as far as Simon is concerned, this is where I'm going to need your help. We are going to blackmail him. He's passed out in bed, you're going to get him undressed, and you too need to be undressed. Lie next to him and I will take pictures, and then with what we do with the pictures I will be able to retire. Putting it another way, me and you will have so much money that we can enjoy the rest of our life."

We go back to the apartment, and Simon is more than passed out. I help Penny take his clothes off. Penny also gets naked. "So how shall we do this?"

"Put your arm and one leg around him and move your face to his face."

"Quick! Hurry! Take the picture, his breath stinks of vomit."

"Ok we need another. Now turn around, spoons position, and I will put his arm around you… perfect. Ok. Got some good shots. Come on, let's go into the kitchen."

"Why don't you send them to Kelly?"

"No, I'm not going to stoop to their level. Besides this would kill her. I know what Kelly's like."

"Yeah, but look at what she's done to you."

"Yes you're right, but I also believe Simon when he said that he loves her. He told me earlier he met someone and that it was the real deal so let them be happy. I'm happy I got you and I'm thinking of the children, and not my feelings. I'm so tired. Let's go to sleep, Pen, we can go in the girls' room. There's no bed in there, just a blow up. Tomorrow's going to be a long day."

"Mike… Mikey, wake up. I hear movement in your bedroom."

"What time is it?"

"It's 10 am."

"Ok, let's go. Just put this sheet around you, walk in the bedroom and say 'morning', sit on the bed and say you had a fun night. I will be right behind you." Penny walks into the bedroom; Simon is sitting on the end of the bed with his head in his hands.

"Morning sweetie," Penny says, as she touches his head. "What a fun evening."

He looks up at me. "Who the hell is that?"

"It's the girl you brought back from the bar last night. Don't you remember?"

"No, no way…I wouldn't… I didn't…"

"Yes you did mate. I got the pictures. I took them on your iPhone to prove it, look." I show him the photos.

"Really, I don't remember a thing."

"I told you the weed was good."

"I don't remember fucking her. Listen Mike, please, this must not be mentioned at all."

"Yeah, no problem mate."

"Listen I got to make a call on your phone. I lost mine last night, that's how drunk we were." I dial Kelly's number and put it on speakerphone.

"Hello Simon."

"No Kelly, it's not Simon, it's your husband."

"Oh, what's the matter Simon? You've gone all white again. Listen you two…Kelly you're right, I do know about you and Simon's affair. Now listen to me. The children won't find out about your nasty little secret but you have to wait for six months until this man…man…piece of shit sets one foot in my house again. I want a divorce straight away, and you don't take half of everything. You will get maintenance for

98

the kids, you get to live in the house until all three kids leave, then you leave, and Simon may never, *ever* live in my house. I don't want to speak to you. The next time we talk will be through my lawyer. You can tell the kids that we are not getting back together and I will arrange for the kids to come and stay next weekend." And with that, I hang up the phone and chuck it to Simon.

"And as for you, mate, it's a good thing I haven't knocked your fucking head off! The deal we just put together is all mine. You sign over 100 percent to me and these pictures will never get emailed to Kelly. Now get the fuck out of my place and you better make sure you look after that woman. You hurt her, fuck anyone else, or fuck with my kids I will hurt you bad." I grab him and push him out of the front door followed by his clothes.

"Are you ok?"

"Yes, I'm fine. So what now?"

"What do you mean what now?"

"Well what are we going to do?"

"We, my lovely sugar tits, are going to enjoy the rest of our week as Penny Snow and Mr. Taylor, and continue our journey."

"What next on our journey then?"

"Well, next stop my dear, is the porn movie. Did you see how good I was at directing those shots?"

"It wasn't exactly that hard, the man was passed out."

"You cheeky thing! Come here, kiss me, and tell me you love me."

"I love you Mike. I love you Mikey. And I love you Michael."

Chapter Thirteen

I really can't believe this has happened to me. So many emotions come over me, exactly like the feelings I felt whilst I was on the plane leaving London to Amsterdam. Sad ones, angry ones, confused ones, disappointed ones, a whole mixture of emotions. Even a slight sigh of relief and even a happy emotion comes over me. So you know what? Today I'm not going to dwell on all the above apart from the happy emotion.

"Penny?"

"Yes, Mike?"

"No more sadness today. Today we are forgetting about everything apart from being happy. No word of anything that is remotely sad, ok?"

"OK Mike. That sounds like a good idea. I'm definitely up for no more tears."

"So what are you suggesting?"

"I'm suggesting today we plan our movie."

"Movie? What movie?"

"Yes, that's right, our porn movie."

"Ok, well Mike, I have to tell you something. This is actually one thing that I haven't explored. Of course watching, but never made one."

"That's fantastic! I'm glad about that, because for once you can't boss me about Ms. Snow. So how do we go about making this porn movie?"

"I'm not sure," Penny says.

"Get a pen and paper Penny. You're going to have to take notes. Let's do a wish list of the things we will need to do, ok?"

Porn title
Porn story line
Scenes
Number of girls
Number of guys
Locations
Clothes
Make up artist
Toys
Camera men
Cameras
Technical stuff
Production crew
Lights
Sound

"Can you think of anything else Penny?"

"No, not really. I don't think so…"

"I'm sure we will think of things as we get going."

"Oh I know! What about catering? The stars need to eat, right," Penny says. I guess we are doing a big production, it's not just me and you with a hand held camera that we can upload to the Internet. Although that does sound good, and a lot easier to do. Doesn't it Mike?"

"No Penny, come on. We are going to do a proper production. Anyone can pick up a camcorder and film people fucking. I want this to be the real deal. I imagine a big production, the best porn stars only. I think we're better off dividing our work. If you wouldn't mind, Pen, could I work on porn title up to toys, and you work on the production side so cameramen up to sound?"

"Ok that sounds like a plan."

"I will work here in the living room and you Ms. Snow shall take the kitchen table."

With that we both jump up and take a serious stance. Penny straight away gets her paper and pen, laptop and the telephone and straight away starts making calls to production houses, whilst me it takes me longer to get motivated. I have no idea what I'm doing, or where to begin. I just stare at the paper reading my notes over and over again. I have no inspiration, so I ring Dick.

"Hi Dick, can you please go and buy me a few different sex movies?"

"Come again?"

"You know, porn movies."

"I know what you mean, that's why I said 'come again'."

"Ah yeah, very funny. Well Dick, I'm afraid to tell you stick to your day job. Jokes are not for you. Anyway, I need porn films, Dick, I'm making a movie."

"Ok no problem. Leave it to me. In fact, why don't you borrow my collection? I only have about five but they are here in the car. I will bring them straight up, ok?"

"Well if you don't mind, that would be great." Porn movies in the car? What the hell would Dick want with porn movies in his car? Oh gosh, I hate to think.

Dick brings his movies up, and I get a cup of tea and set up the DVD player. Four very interesting titles: *European Union of MILF Sluts*, *Ibiza Sex Party*, *Pirates*, and *I Only Luv Girl on Girl*.

What a strange collection, but hey who I am to judge right? Away I know MILF is not for me, I can just tell by the cover. Older looking ladies are not my thing.

"Penny what's a MILF?"

She looks it up on the Internet, a MILF is a "mum I like to fuck". Ok, definitely not my thing. I'm only watching it for research purposes, so I put the film on and write down the facts. It's a 90-minute film with five scenes and nothing much impresses me with this film. They have got it so wrong there are so many MILFs in the world that are absolutely bloody gorgeous. In fact, I wonder what is considered a MILF? Is it a woman over 30?

"Penny what age is considered to be a MILF?"

"A woman between 30 to 45." She continues, "A cougar is an experienced woman."

"Ok, thanks Pen." Too much information. Yes, so this film is not a true likeness of a MILF, so this is in the No pile. Nothing I liked, nothing sexy, nothing that is going to get my dick hard, that's for sure, so no inspiration for my movie in this one.

Next I put on *Ibiza Sex Party*. This is more like it! Again, taking notes: hot girls, amazing location in Ibiza, outdoor fucking in swimming pools. I like this film a lot and my dick is actually starting to get hard watching this, so this one is in the Yes pile. I'm actually starting to paint a picture in my head about my movie now that I've seen this one.

Then the next movie is *Pirates*. Looks really high budget, completely different to the other covers. In fact the cover reminds me of a mainstream movie. Silly me, it's a parody of "Pirates of the Caribbean". Again, good looking girls, good sex scenes. Not that

I know what makes a good sex scene, but again there is movement in my pants, so it must be good. Although, the acting is really bad, it's definitely not going to win any Oscars for Best Actress unless they have awards for Best Orgasms, so this film is a Yes and a No.

Then the last movie is the *I only luv*. Gosh, it's that British female director again, Ionie Luv Coxxx. Apparently she has never starred in any films, although she looks as if she should with a nice body and a very sexy accent.

Her style of directing is different from the other films; she has a cameraman that films her filming and directing. She leaves her voice on camera as she directs the porn scenes. Her twist is actually quite genius-- reality porn. She goes up to real random people on the streets, not porn stars and asks them if they would like to be in her movie, some say yes, some say no. Hard-ons and floppy ones all caught on her camera.

So after my film research and my notes, I'm still no closer to deciding what my porn movie is going to be about. There was something in every movie apart from the MILF that I liked. Then it hits me! That's it. That's it! I have it! The movie should be inspired by all the stuff that I have experienced with Miss Penny Snow. That's it!

"Penny, our movie is going to be based on the sexual experiences I have had with you. We will have a blow job scene, an anal scene, a threesome, a gang-bang scene, and girl on girl. What do you think?"

"Yes I think that sounds good. As one of our locations we could even use the window."

"Yes that would be good. Brilliant Penny! I'm so exited about this movie. So what have you found out?"

104

"Well I managed to find this guy called The Nige. He provides everything we need for the production. He will even edit the film for us and make the cover. He also has connections if we wanto sell it online and in stores if we want to go down that road. What? What are you laughing at mister?"

"I'm not."

"Yes you are, come on what's so funny?"

"Well it's not really funny, it's just your face. You have taken the job description so seriously, then you find a guy with the name The Nige." With that Penny burst out laughing.

"Hey Pen, how about we give each other porn names? What do you think? I read somewhere that a porn name is the name of your pet and the name of your street, so mine would be Bali ColdBrook."

"What is a Bali ColdBrook?" That's not a porn name, that's shit."

"It was the name of my cat and the name of the street I grew up on. Ok Ms. Snow, what would yours be?"

"Well I didn't have a pet, but always wanted a rabbit called Buster. So Stoofsteeg, Buster."

"Stoofsteeg, Buster, that's just as shit as mine."

"No it's not actually. Stoofsteeg is the street where my window is. Stoofsteeg Buster is totally a porn name Mister Bali ColdBrook."

"We have our porn names, production sorted, locations, now all we need is Porn Stars." Stoofsteeg Buster has also sorted that apparently.

"I have found the sexiest, nastiest and horniest." With that she hands me a printout of 15 gorgeous girls with every race practically covered and another sheet with well-endowed men, again every race covered.

105

So now we are complete, we have our production. All I need to do is plot the scenes and decide on how I'm going to direct. After watching the films Dick gave me, I definitely decided that there would be no acting in my films, just a lot of sucking and fucking and my directing approach would be like that of Ms. Ionie luv Coxxx, I'm going to leave my voice on camera. In fact, "Penny, how do you feel about me and you being the narrative directors of the movie? We direct the action live rather than stopping, that way it will be real, a horny couple getting off on the action."

"Yes that sounds good. I like the sound of that."

"Now who's taking the job seriously?"

"I know, who would of thought it?" What's it going to be called?"

"I'm not sure yet, I have a working title. 2 ½ Weeks. It's a parody of 9 ½ Weeks."

"That's crap. Let's choose the name after we finish the film."

"OK Ma'm."

"Well it's been a very long day, shall we get some food and hit the hay?"

"It's 9:30 already? Shit! We've been working on this all day. Where does the time go?"

"I know, tell me about it. Time flies when you're having fun. What's our start time tomorrow Mike?"

"Eight a.m. First location I figured could be Dick's car. Two naughty hitchhikers girls with their backpacks and short skirts could be hitching a ride and we stop to give them a lift, but they have to suck of our friend for the free ride.

"Only one flaw in that scene, it's cold outside."

"Yes I thought of that too, that's why the temperature of the car will be really high so they will have to take their clothes off."

"What an original idea! Bali ColdBrook you're so silly and typical."

"Oh I am? Am I Ms. Stoofsteeg Buster? Well we will see when it's your turn. You can decide on the next scene."

"Ok I will, and you will see."

"Ooh fighting talk. I love it."

Actually thinking about it, I suppose the difference between a woman's' porn thinking and a mans' must be completely different so it should make for a good film.

"Right, food and bed." That's if I can at all sleep. I'm actually too excited about the film. And my mind is doing overtime. What do I do if my cock gets hard? How will I control myself? Well I suppose me and Penny can always sneak off for a quickie.

"Can I speak to all actors involved in Scene 1, please? That includes you too Buster. So this scene is in the car, there will be myself in the driving seat Penny in the passenger. Penny will also be holding a camera to film and Mark… is that your name?"

"Yes it is."

"Mark, you will be sitting in the back fully dressed. You two girls will be standing on the side of the road with your thumbs out. We will stop the car and you ask for a ride. Where you want to go is further than we are driving, so you plead with us, then Mark you also plead with us, so we agree and as a thank you you start sucking Mark off. It's probably best that you sit either side of the car; we will direct you on camera. We will try to not stop unless there is a technical fault. Right Nige?"

"Yep that's correct," Nige jumps in. "Girls it's going to be quite tight in the car, so camera friendly angles please."

The Nige was not what I expected to look like at all. For some reason in my head I thought he would look like a perverted character wearing a rainMac, you know the Mac in the cop TV show Colombo? He was famous for wearing that Mac. Anyhow that's how I imagined The Nige. Not a shaved head guy with a ginger beard, glasses, and an Englishman. Gosh it's strange what we imagine when we don't know. The Nige explained to me and Penny all the lingo that we needed to know so that the cameramen and Pornstars understood. I must say a very good teacher.

"Quiet on set please! Standing by. Rolling. Ok and… Action!" As I slam the clapper board in front of the camera and say, "Scene One Hitchhiking Blow Job."

"Cut! Cut! Stop cameras!"

"What's wrong Nige? Did I say something wrong?"

"No you were perfect Mike, it's just it has started to rain. I'm getting rain on my camera it won't look good."

"So what do we do?"

"Well, we will have to wait until it stops."

"No, I've got a good idea," Penny says. "Let's shoot an alternative scene just in case it doesn't stop raining. My suggestion would be that we have all girls on set. We take the scene into the bedroom of the house and all the girls rotate so one girl starts off sucking Mark, then two girls, then three girls, then they swap out and we keep going like that." Mark nods his head. Yes, please!

"You lucky bugger! Penny can I not do this scene?"

"No this one must be for the pro, you will come too quickly."

"You cheeky cow," I say, as I slap her arse. "And what is our role in this one Penny?"

"Well I will have the camera…"

"And I can talk to Mark."

"What are you going to say?"

"I don't know, I will improvise. And you have the other Camera and do what I say."

"Like I always do."

"Now, now, children, let's get this scene done, you can argue after," says The Nige.

"Everybody ready? Let's try it again. Quiet on set! Standing by. Standing by. Rolling… and Action!"

Mark is lying in the bed pretending to be asleep. "Wakey, wakey birthday boy. I have a big surprise for you."

Mark opens his eyes and looks at the camera. "Oh you do?"

"I do indeed! I have 15 girls to suck your big, juicy cock."

"Where did you get 15 girls?"

"Well my friend, Mr. Bali ColdBrook acquired them whilst on vacation."

"I sure did and I tell you they're hot!"

"Bali ColdBrook, why don't you show the girls into the room?"

"Come on ladies, you have a big one waiting for those juicy mouths. I want to see you suck that cock nice and hard. That's it, ladies, come and sit on the bed. Why don't you with the big tits wank birthday boy's cock a little bit, get it nice and juicy for the other girls. What do you think Bali ColdBrook?"

"Yeah I think that's a great idea, Stoofsteeg Buster. Yeah I like the way she's rubbing her tits on his cock, that's getting it hard. Is it getting hard Mark?"

"Yes it's really hard."

"So come on girls, start sucking it. Really feel his cock in your mouth, devour it, kiss it, eat it like you have never eaten anything before."

"Why don't I bring in two more girls Stoofsteeg Buster?"

"That sounds like a great idea, Bali ColdBrook, they can kiss Mark."

"Do you think you could also touch my cock a little? I'm getting a little jealous watching all these girls do Mark," Mike says.

"I sure can, come here." I put my camera down and Penny puts hers down as the cameramen carry on filming. Penny starts to rub me outside of my trousers. Shit I'm so turned on. This is so horny with beautiful girls sucking cock. Before you know it, there are two girls kissing Mark, two girls kissing each other, and three girls fighting for his cock. We don't have to actually give much direction; everything just seems to be happening naturally.

"Gosh Penny", I whisper, "I'm so turned on."

"Well why don't you join in?"

"I can?" I say, surprised.

"Yes why not?" Penny picks up her camera. "Oh ladies, I think you need another cock as one is not enough. My naughty partner in crime is going to join you. Come on Bali ColdBrook, let these three beauties pleasure you."

Oh wow! This is intense. "That's it suck on my balls," I say.

110

"Come on put them all in your mouth. Oh you greedy girl! Does that feel good? Look into my camera."

You have no idea how good it feels. "Maybe the other two girls should share your cock," says Penny. "That's it girls, go on let me see you gag on his cock. Come on, deeper, put it deeper into your mouths."

"Oh, no, no," Mike whispers.

"What's wrong?"

"I don't want to come yet."

"It's okay Mike."

"Yes, come! Let me see you come into their mouths. Girls, once he's come into your mouths, I want you to show the camera."

"Ok, here I go. Ready girls? I'm going to fill you up. Oh shit! Here I come."

Penny shouts, "That's it. Quick, suck him harder!"

"Agh yes yes yes em"

"That looks good ladies. Look at me show me all that juice. Very nice. And how is Mark doing? Oh yeah I see you're close to coming too. I think you should come over some hot arses. Whose arse do you think Mark should come on, Bali ColdBrook?"

"Oh I think those two arses, they look like they need some hot come in them."

"So when you're ready Mark, you can come." Probably a big mistake to tell the actor in his own time he could come, he went on and on until all 15 girls had sucked him off. I suppose it was some industry thing to add on to his curriculum vitae, that he had 15 girls, and he kept going for an hour.

Boy that was a long scene. I only intended on the film being 90-minutes. Maybe this will have to be the bonus blow-job scene.   In fact this could be the film.

"Cut cameras!   Well done everybody, great scene.   30 minute break then Scene 2."

"So how was that Nige?"

"That was hot. I mean you two talking to each other made the scene a big turn on, especially your voice Penny. Even though it was an hour long fucking hot, I will be sad to edit that down."

"Well we should keep it as a bonus scene."

"That sounds like a good idea."

"So where's the next scene and I'll get the boys to set it up," The Nige says.

"Well I thought the kitchen. What do you think Penny? As you did a good job on that scene, you can plot the second scene."

"I already did. I'm way ahead. This is the threesome, right?"

"Right. I think you should have the natural blonde with the real tits and two guys, a black guy and a white guy.   That will look real hot and there should definitely be DP in this scene."

"What's DP?"

"Double penetration. That's where it's anal and pussy sex at the same time."

"It's a tricky position," The Nige says. "The only way that act will look good on camera is if one guy lies on his back, the girl straddles him but lying on her back too. That way he can touch her clit and boobs and he can enter her arse then the other guy can fuck her normal, I mean missionary. We get a great view of both holes being fucked and only one camera needs to cover that area, and the other camera can focus on face and boobs."

"Ok sounds good."

"I'll go check on the boys."

"Penny, how you feeling?"

"I'm feeling great. I'm really getting into the role."

I can see that. Are you sure you were okay about me jumping in? I couldn't help myself it was such a turn on."

"I didn't mind at all. I was turned on myself by watching the pleasure on your face. In fact, we should borrow one of the cameras and film ourselves."

"Yeah let's do that. I wonder if it's stopped raining yet?"

"Nope it hasn't, it's bloody pissing down."

"Oh well. It looks like we will use all the rooms in the house after all."

"I hope not, I want my outdoor scenes in."

"Ok guys, we're ready. Everyone's on set. You explain this one, Mike."

"No probs. Right guys, this scene I want to be quite sensual. Even though it's DP I want Natalie to guide you, she is a goddess and your worshipping her. So make it very romantic, lots of kissing, kissing of the neck, kissing her bum and worshiping her whole body. Again, I don't think this scene should start with both guys. Let's just use one, and then the other guy can come in once Natalie is in total ecstasy, because at that point she is going to want more. Do you agree Penny?"

"Yes I do. Natalie this scene is all about you, so I don't think you should spend too much time giving them blowjobs. I want this scene to be for the women."

"I don't think we should direct on camera, obviously we will speak and direct, but Nige can you take our voices out of this scene."

"Yep no problem."

With this scene I think we should just let the passion flow, as this scene is a dream sequence. Natalie, you're on the computer on a dating site looking at all the hot men. You start playing with yourself, and then the guys appear. Can we do that, Nige?"

"Yes, we can make it look like a dream in the edit, just take all the action very slow. Ok everyone clear? Ok quiet on set. Lights, camera and action."

"That's it Natalie, those hot men are turning you on, so reach for your pussy. In fact, you should make yourself come before Leo comes in."

This scene is really hot and different from the last one. Real passionate. The first scene was horny and filthy, what you expect from a porn movie, but this scene is so romantic. I know they're acting but in this scene I really believe they're not, and enjoying it.

Penny did a good job with the actors. She found out what everybody liked, what their sexual strengths were, and what they were happy doing. She felt that if she found out that information it would make for a better movie, as they would be into it and enjoy it and she was right. Again not much direction was needed in this film.

Leo started kissing the whole of Natalie's body, he actually had her facedown and worked his way up from her feet to her bum with gentle strokes and kisses and licks. He then moves up to her neck, kisses her neck, and then turns her over so he is now kissing her face. He slowly moves his tongue down to her boobs where he stops for a while, then slowly to her pussy, and stays there until she comes.   He thrusts inside her, they take turns being on top. Natalie comes again and Leo goes down on her to lick her again. Whilst he's licking her, Tommy comes in and Natalie starts to suck Tommy to get him nice and hard.   Natalie comes again and says to the boys that she wants them both inside her. They both try and fuck her pussy but Leo keeps falling out, so Nige calls cut. "Sorry about that guys, I know you were on a roll, but I think it would be easier if we get in to the DP position now, I will just fade it in."

So they get into the position and start fucking, one in the pussy one in the arse.   It really does look great and Natalie seems to be enjoying it, and so does Penny. They carry on in this position only for five minutes, as it's a very hard position. They stop before it all goes wrong. The Nige calls it. It's time for come, come on demand. "Ok boys, time to come."

Shit, that's crazy. How can they do that? I suppose that's their job. I know I couldn't come on demand. The scene ends with all three coming together. And we all give a big round of applause.

"Great guys! That was fantastic."

"Yeah it was."

"Natalie?"

"Yes, Penny?"

"Is that really a hard position to do?"

"Yeah it is. It takes some practice.   The trick is to stay very still and let the guys do all the work, because if you jiggle around too much they end up slipping out of you."

"Oh, I see.   Well it looked good on camera. Do you mind me asking you another question?"

"No, go ahead."

"Why did you choose this career path?"

"Erm…good question.   It was my boyfriend, he was a porn star and he was doing a film called *Real Couples*. I went along to watch, and the producer asked if I had ever thought about doing it. I said no. He said it was a shame as I look good and it would be really good filming a real couple rather than pretending. The girl my boyfriend was doing the scene with turned up completely drunk and on drugs, so the scene was going to be dropped, so I said I would do it.   At first I was nervous, but I was having sex with my boyfriend.   The only difference was the cameras, but I forgot they were there. I really loved it, and realized that I was an exhibitionist and couldn't get enough. 43 scenes later, here I am. Still loving it and I love sex too, so it's an added bonus because my job gives me so much pleasure."

"Have you had any sex scenes you haven't enjoyed?"

"I don't really enjoy girl on girl. I don't mind receiving from a girl, but giving back is not my thing. I like women, but sexually they do nothing for me. I'm definitely all for a cock."

"Yep it definitely shows. Well nice meeting you. See you on set tomorrow."

"Mike, I'm so horny after that scene, aren't you?"

"It was very hot. Mind you, I think after every scene I'm going to be horny."

"How about we call it a day now, as it's already six o'clock and ask the Nige to film you and me?"

"That sounds like a definite plan."

"Ok everyone, that's a wrap for today, see you all tomorrow same time. Don't forget we are in different locations so if you could show up an hour before your call time, please."

"Hey Mike, how come you are calling it early? We still have one more scene."

"I know mate, but me and Penny would like to do a scene ourselves. What do you say Nige, you up for filming me and the lovely Ms. Snow?"

"I don't see why not. Can I be director?"

"Yea, that would be good. That way we get the porn star experience. As long as there is no come on demands, that's something for the professionals."

"No, it's all in your mind. Fucking is all in the head you can control it, believe me."

"I'll take your word for it. I am happy to let Ms. Snow control me."

"Ok, I will go set up. Penny should go to makeup, and you could do with a bit of bronzer too."

"What?"

"I'm only joking, but you did say you wanted the porn star experience."

"Very funny, Nige. Penny, go into makeup, I'm just going to check my phone."

"OK, see you soon Mike."

I turn on my phone and see five missed calls, all from Kelly. I listen to my answer phone. "Michael, it's me, Kelly. I'm so very sorry. I know you don't want to speak to me. I know you are hurt and upset."

Hurt and upset? That's an understatement. You have been fucking my work colleague. I can find more words than hurt or upset! As I go to put the phone down, I hear baby Amber in the background of the voicemail so I carry on to listen. "Please Mike, I need to speak to you not on the phone. Face-to-face. I have told the kids and they're pretty upset as you can imagine. They want to see you. In fact, they hate me for what I have done. Rachel won't talk to me. Please Mike…"

I hang up the phone. Shit! You know what, if it wasn't for the kids I would leave that woman to rot. You hear about it all the time, men cheating on their wives. Over the years I've had my chances, but I never did. I married Kelly 'till death do us part'. I'm the first to admit marriage is hard, and me and Kelly have had our struggles but I never ever in a million years thought she was capable of this. It just goes to show that it is not all men that cheat; it's women too.

"Penny, sweetheart. I'm so sorry, but we can't do our scene, we will have to finish it another day. It's the children. Kelly has told them. I need to go back to London. Please understand if it wasn't for them I wouldn't go back."

"Mike, you don't have to explain. Of course I understand. I will gather up our belongings and explain it to The Nige."

"We will finish it another day, I promise."

"I know we will."

Chapter Fourteen

Dick picks us up from the location and drives us back to the apartment. This time I'm the one that's quiet in the car, I think it's finally sunk in. Shit! I feel like shit, I actually want to cry again but I hold it together, not because I'm being macho in front of Penny, I just don't feel I want to give Kelly and that bastard Simon the satisfaction.   Fuck him! How could he do this to me? He was my fucking friend. He was my business partner.

"Mike are you ok? I'm sorry you're sad. I'm sorry this has happened to you. What can I do? Can I help you in any way?"

"Penny, darling you are helping me in more ways than you can imagine."

"Well, I've got something to cheer you up. You know the girl in the last scene, Natalie? She quite fancied you.   She said you look like the actor Jonathan Rhys Meyers from the TV series *The Tudors.*"

"Wow, she said that? That definitely is a compliment, don't you think? I do."

"Indeed, I don't actually know who he is. But to me you look like Rob Lowe, he is so hot. Anyway, all you need to know is that you are very good looking, sexy, and you're my man. You might not be skillful in bed yet but you're enthusiastic so that makes up for it."

"Oh is that so miss? All these cheeky comments! You need bending over my knee."

"I do, do I?"

"See, at least now I've got a smile from you. I'm joking. I love making love to you. You are more than skillful. I know this sounds stupid, but you fit so well inside me and it feels so good."

"Well that is a good thing."

"Mike, I want to support you. I'm coming to London with you."

"No Penny. You don't have to."

"Yes I want to. Please."

"How can you? I know we were not going to talk about it, but is it safe for you to travel? Surely you can be found by using your passport."

"Nope, it's all good. I have a new identity, remember, and with my new identity came a new passport."

"But how?"

"Kitty introduced me to this guy. I have a birth certificate, passport and driving license with Penny Snow so I'm ok to go."

"Ok well, if you are sure I would love for you to come with me. Let me call Amelia so she can book us on the first flight in the morning."

"British Airways flight 2759 is now boarding, could all passengers make their way to the gate, as the gate is now closing."

I don't know if it is déjà vu or what, but this time I'm looking over the dams of Amsterdam as the plane takes off with a beautiful, wonderful woman sitting next to me. So this time I don't feel so sad. We arrive at London Heathrow airport five minutes early.

"Good morning ladies and gentlemen, welcome to London Heathrow where the time is exactly 9 AM in the morning. The outside temperature is 10° warmer than Amsterdam. Have a good day and thank you for flying with British Airways."

In the arrivals hall, Tony greets us. I say, "Hello mate. How you doing? It's so good to see you."

"Yeah you too mate, it seems like you've been gone forever."

"I know, tell me about it it's actually been 11 days but it seems like a lifetime."

"How long are you back for?"

"I'm not sure yet mate. I suppose you heard the news?"

"Yeah we did. Kelly came over last night. I'm so sorry Mike, we had no idea."

"I know, neither did I. If you don't mind Tone, let's not talk about it now."

"Okay, I'm sorry."

"Nothing to be sorry about. I just want to introduce you to someone. Tony meet Miss Penny Snow."

"Wow! You're Penny. I've heard so much about you. Mike told me you were gorgeous, and he wasn't lying."

"Hi Tony. I've heard all about you too. Good to meet you."

"Thanks Tone for coming to pick us up."

"No problem mate. I take it you're staying with Beth and me?"

"Oh I don't know, mate. I don't think I should rub it in Kelly's face. I think we will just check into the hotel around the corner."

"Ok if you're sure. Actually, I'm not thinking properly as Beth doesn't know anything about Penny. So it's probably a good idea."

We drive all the way to London catching up on the football, and reminiscing on old times. "Here we are. The Marriott."

"It is the best hotel around here, Penny, and it's within walking distance from my house. Didn't you do the upgrade on the rooms Tone?"

"Yeah I did mate. In fact you should stay in the Princess Suite. It's really nice and has a massive hot tub."

"Yeah that sounds good. Good idea Tone. Thanks for the lift mate, so good to see you. Hopefully we will see you later."

"I'm on the blower mate. Nice meeting you Penny."

"Yes, same to you Tony."

Mike turns to Penny. "So here we are, London."

"I love it Mike. What a lovely place. London has so much culture. The buildings are amazing."

"Yes London is a very special place, full of character. You should take a look around, go and visit the Houses of Parliament and Big Ben. The Tower of London is good. My girls love to go there."

"Isn't that where Henry VIII lived?"

"No it's where Henry VIII killed his wives. Did you know the Church of England was a made up church by Henry VIII? He went to the Pope to ask if he could divorce Catherine of Aragon, and marry Anne Boleyn. The Pope said no due to the Catholic religion."

"How interesting. I didn't know that."

"Also Anne Boleyn got beheaded at the Tower of London. I will get you a driver to take you around to all the fun places in London."

"Yes please! I would love to see the Queen. I've seen Buckingham Palace on TV, so to see it close up would be good."

"Ok well that's the plan for Penny Snow today, sightseeing in London town whilst I go and see Kelly."

We check into the hotel and go to the room.

"This is a lovely room Mike."

"Yep it's not bad. The car is coming for you. Have a great London experience and call me when you're done."

"I will. Hey, good luck today. I hope it goes okay and I'm here to support you.   Mike I know it's only been 11 days but you know I love you."

"I know and I love you too."

I walk up to my house and I'm nervous. Why am I so nervous? This is my bloody house! Do I ring the bell? No why should I, it's my house! I let myself in with my keys. I open the door and immediately my nose is hit by a familiar smell, you know the house smell. Everyone has a house smell. My house smell is very perfumey which is not surprising with all the girls in the house.   I walk into the kitchen where Marie the nanny is standing there.

"Hello Marie."

"Hi Mike." She gives me a big hug, "I just put the kettle on do you want a cuppa?"

"Yes please, I would love a cuppa. I've really missed tea even though I do have it in Amsterdam. It's just not the same. So how's things been, Marie?"

"Yeah. Good, baby Amber is adorable."

"I missed her."

"Well I will pick her up early from nursery so you can see her."

"That would be great. And the teenagers?"

"Well, Rachel is not speaking to Kelly. Gemma has been her usual lazy self. So you could say the house is still chaotic."

"Well I can't say I missed that."

"Hello Mike." I turn around and Kelly is standing behind me.

"Excuse me. I'm going to my room and I will leave you two to talk," says Marie.

"Hi Kelly you look good."

"Thanks, Mike. So do you."

"Kelly, in fact, you look really beautiful."

"Thank you Mike. Thank you for coming."

"Kelly I only came because of the girls."

"Mike let's go into the living room please." We go into the living room, I sit down on the sofa and Kelly sits next to me. She grabs my hand holds it to her mouth and kisses it. I pull it away. "Don't Kelly," I say.

"Please Mike, can you listen to me? Please let me speak then say what you will. I'm so sorry. I'm so very sorry. You shouldn't of found out that way. That was wrong."

"You don't fucking say Kelly. The whole thing was wrong."

"I know it was. I was so out of order and I know that what I have done is unforgivable. I owe you the truth. I do love you Mike."

"You have a good way of showing it, Kelly."

"My love for you turned into a brother type of love. We were so young, Mike, our lives have flashed in front of our eyes. Gosh where do I begin?"

"I don't know Kelly, you tell me."

"Ok. Remember six months ago when I was really depressed about my weight? All you did was work and football, bloody football. You hardly noticed me, we never went out."

124

"Yes but that was because we have a small child."

"No Mike. We drifted apart. We drifted apart years ago, then Amber came along and it made our situation worse because now all the focus was on her. I fell into the background. You started taking me for granted. I'm a woman. I still want flowers, I still want romance, I still want to be wowed, I still want the flirty stuff. Being spontaneous and all that went, and it went ages ago. It's not like we didn't try Mike, we went to marriage counseling. You stopped putting effort in. You made me feel not special, you made me feel second best, work and football before me. I even get jealous of how much time you spend with the girls, how much attention you give them and me nothing. You didn't... don't notice me. I told you time and time again how I wanted to be treated and you never took me seriously."

"That's not true Kelly."

"It is Mike. I'm the one living it. Then the last straw was when you forgot our wedding anniversary this year. How could you? It broke my heart."

"I know Kelly, but we made up for me forgetting and had a nice time didn't we?"

"Well actually, no we didn't. The day I came to your office and we were going to go for lunch at the last minute you canceled. It was too late. I was already at the office. Do you remember that Simon took me for lunch? That's when it started. We started talking about Simon and his situation with Sarah, and immediately it sounded familiar, it was our relationship. Simon asked me not to tell anyone as he and Sarah wanted to tell the girls first. Simon and I would meet once a week and just talk, that's all. He complimented me, made me feel alive and young again. I liked the attention. You didn't even notice.

You couldn't even tell when I had my hair done. I wanted to tell you three months in, but I couldn't. I thought we must stay together because of the kids, and whilst Simon was around it made you bearable. The whole Amsterdam thing was wrong. I just couldn't find a way of telling you. I suppose I took the coward's way out."

"Yes you did Kelly."

"I just thought you would go to Amsterdam, and we would drift more apart. It would have been easier for you to handle. Like I said, I had no intention of you finding out the way you did. It was wrong of me and Simon to set you up like that. I honestly thought and was hoping you would meet someone else, but you're such a good guy, a good person, you wouldn't do that to me. I suppose that's one good thing about you Mike, you might not have been the romantic but you're an honest guy."

"Kelly, stop. I had no idea I behaved like that. Why didn't you make me listen to your needs?"

"I tried to Mike. I did try. Like I said, you have been in a world of your own. It doesn't excuse my behavior, but that's why women and men meet someone else. It's not rocket science Mike."

"Yeah, I suppose you are right. Kelly, I did meet someone."

"What?" Kelly then starts crying. "You bastard! You hypocrite!"

"No Kelly. No, no you don't. I tried to tell you on the phone two days ago, but you cut me off and said you were going to ring me back and you didn't. Remember? Also Kelly, when I moved to Amsterdam you were the one who wanted a break, a separation, so I didn't cheat on you like you have done to me."

126

"Well me and Simon have not had sex together yet because I wanted to wait until I told you."

"But on your message you said you loved him."

"I do Mike. It doesn't mean you have to have sex with someone to love them."

"Oh great, Kelly turn it all on me, if that's what you want. I'm the shit here, am I? I'm the one that is conniving and goes plotting behind her husband's back to be with her lover. Mine was an accident, not planned. An accident and I have been feeling so guilty about it. The strange thing is Kelly, I do love you, I still do. I'm not in love with you but you are the mother of my three lovely children, so I always will."

"Yes you're right, I suppose, for me too the love changed. I'm not sure I would say it's the same love, but it has changed. Is she nice?"

"Who? Is who nice?"

"The woman you have met."

"Yes. She is very nice."

"So how did you meet her?"

"It's a long story Kelly. Let's not talk about it please."

"Why not?"

"Because its irrelevant. You don't need to know the details."

That's why you were MIA for the first few days, was it?"

"Yes it was Kelly, this will get us nowhere. You want to be with Simon. Are you sure about that?"

"Do you want to be with your girl?"

127

"Penny. Her name is Penny. I think so Kelly, I have fallen for her. I actually have fallen in love with her. Gosh Kelly, what a mess all this is. We have three children, that's why it's important we do the right thing."

"Look Mike, please. Let's forgive each other. Please for once let's make each other happy. Let's do it for the children."

"Well at least let us try." We spend the next four hours talking about how we are going to move forward, how we would share the kids and we even looked at old photos and laughed.

"Mike?"

"Yes Kelly?"

"Can we have a hug?"

"Yes." We hold each other tight. The long hug goodbye turns into a kiss, a passionate one then we cry together.

"Ok Kelly, I'm going to go to nursery and pick Amber up. I will also pick up the girls too."

"Mike why don't you stay here tonight? The girls would love it."

"I don't know. I have Penny in the Marriott."

"Bring her here."

"No, I think it's too soon for all of that, besides I want to make Rachel understand."

"I know she hates me."

"Why Kelly? What did you say?"

"I told her the truth. After all she is 16."

"Well I will repair the damage for you."

"Thank you."

"Kelly, I'm sorry it's ended like this."

"Me too."

"You know Simon is a really good guy."

"I know he is and I really like him Mike."

"I know you do. Be happy. Go on, go see him and have your first romantic night."

128

I cannot believe I just said that. OMG I just told my wife to go and have sex with her lover. I'm not right in the head.

"I'm so glad we sorted things out and we can be good friends Mike."

"I know we can. Go on, off you go." I give her a kiss on the forehead and she grabs her car keys and leaves the house. Shit did all that really happen? I do feel sad, but I want Kelly to be happy. I obviously can't and Simon will. I do feel better knowing that she hasn't slept with Simon yet.

"Marie, if you don't mind I'm going to pick up the kids from school."

"Ok Mike, are you ok?"

"Yes I'm fine. Kelly and I have sorted things out so it's all amicable."

"Oh that's great."

"Thank goodness."

I pick up the girls from school and we go get food and ice cream. We have a real good time and they were so pleased to see me and I was to see them. I bathe Amber, read her a story and put her to bed. I then have the talk with the teenagers and make them understand what had happened. I tell them they are not to blame their mum. I also tell them that I had met someone, and the first thing Gemma wanted to know was when she could meet her. Surprisingly they both took it well and understood. "Right girls, I think it's bedtime don't you? School tomorrow and I'm out of sync. Once again, the usual bedtime chaos starts as they fight over the shower. I actually laugh to myself and let them fight it out between themselves. They soon work it out and go to bed. I then ring Penny.

"Hello Pen."

"Hey Mike.   How did it go?"

"It was as you could imagine very sad, but we have sorted things out, so it's all good. I also told her about you."

"How did that go down?"

"Well not good at first then it was ok. We had a cry, a hug, even a kiss."

"Well I'm glad it worked out."

"Yeah so am I.   Anyway how was your day?"

"Oh Mike it was fantastic! I love London! What an amazing city. I watched the changing of the guards at Buckingham Palace, I even went on the London Eye. You can see the whole of London from there.   I bought a book on the history of London, and I'm looking forward to reading it."

"That's great Penny. I'm here with the kids as Kelly is over at Simon's so I'm staying here tonight. It's been so good to see them. I've missed them."

"Oh good, I'm glad you had a good time. I'm not back at the hotel yet, I stopped at Nobu to have sushi. One thing I miss about America is we have good sushi.   They don't have to many places in Amsterdam."

"Nobu is expensive."

"Yea it is but it is so good. I'm going to read my London book when I get back to the hotel. What do you think you will do tomorrow?"

"Take the kids to school in the morning then come get you. Kelly and I have sorted everything out, so there's no need to speak again.   I'm going to have the kids every other weekend and holidays for now. Either I will fly here or they will fly to me.   Once I'm more settled in Amsterdam I might have Amber over a lot more as she doesn't have to go to school."

"That sounds good."

"So are you all touristed out?"

"Actually I'm not. I would love to go to the country."

"Well I tell you what Ms. Snow, we will have a date. I will pick you up at 930 and we will drive out into the country and have a romantic pub lunch."

"That sounds great, Mike."

"Night Penny. I love you"

"Night Mike. I can't wait to see you tomorrow."

"Me too."

Chapter Fifteen

"Dad, Dad! Wake up Dad!"

"Jesus what time is it?" I jump up startled, look at the alarm clock, which says 08.03. "Oh I'm sorry Gemma, I slept through the alarm clock." The last 10 days or so I haven't really had a routine so I'm out of touch. I'm so sorry."

"That's ok Dad, but I'm going to leave for school now. I have to be early today I have a play meeting. I'm lead in this year's *Charlie Brown* play."

"Gemma that's amazing! Well done sweetheart. You know I'm off, back to Amsterdam tomorrow so I will see you next weekend."

"Ok Dad. Well … love you and I'm glad you and Mum have sorted things out. You will be ok? Won't you Dad?"

"Of course I will. Hey remember what I said, go easy on your Mum and don't give Simon to much of a hard time will you."

"I will try not to Dad."

"Good girl."

I jump out of bed and it feels strange to have no one beside me. What is more than strange is the fact that Kelly is not here, and for once there is no chaos. I'm not sorting out World War Two. I go into Ambers' room. She is wide awake playing quietly in her cot. I call for Marie.

"Marie can you come and get Amber ready?"

"Yes no problem," she shouts. I pick Amber up, give her a big kiss and pass her to Marie. I then look into Rachel's room she's not there. I go down into the kitchen and there she is eating some toast. "Morning darling, how are you this morning?"

"I'm good. Thanks Dad. How are you? Did you sleep ok?"

132

"I did. In fact it was strange in the bed without your Mum but I will get used to it."

"I'm so sorry Dad."

"It's ok Rachel, I will be just fine and Penny is lovely, you will like her. Do you want a lift to school?"

"No thanks. Billy is meeting me."

"Who's Billy?"

"He's sort of my boyfriend."

"Ok. Well I hope …"

"Dad don't say it, I've already had the lecture from Mum. I know your story and how Mum got pregnant at 17. That's why you married her. Don't worry, I'm not having sex."

"That's good to hear," I say as I kiss her goodbye and she leaves hand in hand with Billy. It's a surprisingly nice feeling to know that Rachel has a distraction to take her away from the news of Kelly and my split.

I get showered and dressed then have some food before taking Amber to nursery. I feel ok with leaving, knowing that the girls are fine and that Kelly and I have come to an amicable solution.

I have one last glance at my house and shut the door. I have a few cars but decide I will take Penny Snow out in my old first generation Alfa Romeo. This was the first car I bought when I made some money. I love this car, it's Italian and the perfect-looking car for driving out into the country in, as it looks very James Bond.

I drop Amber off at nursery then pull up outside of the hotel. I ring Penny and tell her to come down to the car. "Good morning," I say.

"Good morning Mike, what a glorious day it is." She gives me a big kiss. "I like the car."

"I thought you might, that's why I choose this one, it has real character to it."

"I agree. Where are we going?"

"I figured a nice easy drive that wasn't too far away and you still get the country feel is Sussex. We are going to go to East Sussex, it will take us about an hour and 45 minutes. There is this great little pub on Devil's Dyke, called the Devil's Dyke Pub."

"Devil's Dyke, that sounds scary. What's Devil's Dyke?"

"Well it's a major local tourist attraction dating far back as the 19th and 20th century. The dyke is a V Shaped valley, the work of the devil. Wikipedia says, as the legend goes, the devil was digging a trench to allow the sea to flood the many churches in the Weald of Sussex. The digging angered a rooster causing it to crow, making the devil believe that the morning was fast approaching. The devil then fled, leaving his trench unfinished. I also heard that the dyke was formed by the devil when he was struck by lightning making the valley split into a v shape. Anyhow, whatever the myth, it's a beautiful place and a great place for lunch and it's one place I have never been before so it should be a nice first experience for both of us."

"Oh it sound so exciting Mike, I can't wait! Can we have the roof down?"

"Yeah, why not? I pull over just a yard from Hammersmith Bridge and pull the roof down. In these old cars you have to manually pull the roof down. Penny also gets out as she wants to have a look at the bridge. "Wow what a beautiful bridge."

"Yes it is. It lights up at night so pretty, and the water underneath is the River Thames."

"Gosh London is such a historical looking place, you can smell the history. It's so unique. Let's have our picture taken." We stop a man and ask him

134

to take our picture. Penny thinks we look like the perfect couple in the picture, as we both look so happy. We get back in the car with the roof down and the wind blowing our hair. It's a nice autumn day today, the sun is shining so not too cold, not to warm, just nice.

"Last night I was watching the news, and a funny story came up," said Penny. "It made me think of you. This member of Parliament was caught coming out of a high society masquerade ball, only it's not really a ball, it was a house of ill repute. One of the girls recognized him as he took his mask off whilst he went down on her."

"So why did that make you think of me?"

"I don't know, it just did. I really want to go there, do you think we could go there? It is on Great Portland Street."

"Ok we shall investigate. First let's enjoy the country air."

"Ok sir."

"Penny, what do you call a motorway?"

"The road we are on now, we call it a freeway."

"Ah that's right, I couldn't remember what the Americans call it."

"Well now you know."

"I do indeed. We need to get of the next exit." We get off at the next exit and straight away we are driving on a country lane still with the roof down, and it is so peaceful. It's a tension release, that's for sure. The last couple of days just disappear I feel really good, and have a quick glance at Penny. I can see from the expression on her face she too is enjoying the scenic ride.

We pull up to the Devil's Dyke Pub. The sign reads, 'Welcome to the Devil's Dyke. Seasonal food in unspoilt surroundings'. The sign was not wrong. We get out of the car and take a moment to look at the view. It is breathtaking. For as far as the eye can see there is a blanket of green. Green trees, green land; it is something really magical. The air from being high up is so clean, crisp and fresh. "Shall we go and look at the dyke before we eat and really work up an appetite?"

"I think that's exactly what we should do."

We walk hand in hand not really talking, just taking in the beautiful surroundings. We get to Devil's Dyke and it is spectacular. We see a deer and butterflies. It's quite overwhelming; nature is a funny thing and how it makes you feel inside. I feel like I have not a care in the world. Connecting with Mother Nature is something I have always laughed at. I'm a city boy. Bloody Mother Nature. Meeting Penny has changed the way I think about a lot of things. I fucked up with my wife, I'm not going to fuck up with Penny. She is for keeps.

"Mike it's so beautiful, I cannot believe you have never been here before."

"I know. I can't believe it either. Let's lay down and just look at the sky."

I wake to Penny kissing me. "Oh, I'm sorry. Did I fall asleep?"

"Yes you did, it must be the fresh air. Look what I made, a daisy chain."

"Oh very nice Penny, you look like a sexy hippy chick."

"I feel like one too. Free and alive." She spins around and around with her hands high above her head.

136

"Well let's take your free and alive ass to lunch.   It's already three in the afternoon and the sun will go down in two hours then it will be pitch black."

We walk back to the pub and order traditional dishes. I have the Beef, Mushroom and Ale Pie, and Penny orders Hunters Chicken and a bottle of white wine. I have one glass as I'm driving, Penny has the rest and then another bottle, so she is yes, you guessed it, a little more than tipsy.

We eat, laugh, talk, and kiss a lot.   The wine has definitely gone to Penny's head.   Women and wine make for a frisky evening so I suggest to Penny we get a room close by instead of the hour 40 minutes back to London, but Penny insisted we go back. I agreed but really all I wanted to do was fuck her now.

"I'm just going to use the ladies' room before we go."

"I will get the bill."

Penny returns a while later.

"You took your time, everything ok?"

"Yes it's fine. I was just talking to a woman in the restroom, and you are not going to believe this Mikey, this area is known for dogging."

"What is that?"

"I know dogging, it's a word.   The lady didn't tell me and when I asked her what it meant, she said 'Oh, I'm sorry,' and walked out. I Googled it on my iPhone and it reads, 'Dogging is a British English euphemism for engaging in sexual acts in public.'

The reason it is called dogging, is because of the excuses men and women would give to their spouses -- they would say that they were taking the dog for a walk."

"No way!"

"Yes way."

"How funny. No wonder Tony takes his dog out for a walk every night at the same time, seven pm on the dot, and gets into a panic if he's three minutes late. Dirty bugger."

"No he doesn't! Does he?"

"I'm telling you Penny, at seven every night over Hampstead Heath. And I've been there when he tells Beth, 'No, no you sit down love. You had a long day, I will take the dog.' And it's funny how he knows a lot about sex." We both start laughing hard.

"How much fun does that sound Mike?"

"It does indeed. Penny, I'm intrigued. What did that woman look like? I will go ask her where it is."

"There, over there. Look that's her."

"Ok. Come on come with me. I will do the talking."

"Excuse me, Miss, I'm sorry to bother you. You couldn't tell me the spot, the place I can walk my dog?"

"Ah yes I can," she replies and winks at me. "If you come out of the pub, do a right and just keep following the road. On the left hand side you will see a picnic area. Pull in drive, a little pass the picnic area and there you will see some cars."

"Ok, thank you," I say, as I wink back. "Come on Pen, let's go dogging."

We get in the car and start driving in the pitch black with only the headlights of the car for light. We drive around the top of the dyke for at least five minutes. "There!" Penny shouts. "Look that's the picnic area."

We pull up and I reverse the car, so we are facing the road and I turn off the engine. We are now sitting in compete darkness. "Now what?" Penny whispers.

138

"Why are you whispering," I say. "I don't know, I suppose it's dark and scary."

"Well how would I know what happens," I whisper back. I notice that there are four other cars with their lights and engines off. The next minute a bright orange saloon car enters the picnic area. The headlights of the car go off and are replaced by an interior light. The car then parks, a woman in her late 30s with dark hair begins to start kissing a grey-haired man that is in the driving seat. The interior light of the car floodlights the couple so you can see everything.

The woman takes off her top to reveal her huge breasts and the old man starts sucking on them. A young man in the car next to us in his early twenties gets out of the car, shouts out 'whoop whoop', crosses the car park and stands by the passenger side of the car and just watches. The lady is now sucking off the old guy, and another two men, a grey-haired guy and a fat guy also surround the car. The younger guy puts his face onto the glass of the passenger window and starts to rub his crotch on the outside of his jeans. He unzips the jeans, reaches inside and I do believe he is wanking. Me and Penny don't say a word, I'm just in disbelief in what I am seeing. I would not of thought of this in a million years. Mind you, all the sexual experiences I have experienced in the last 10-11 days have been mind blowing. "Penny what do you think?"

"It's a real turn on, the fact that we are in pitch black, the setting, the cars, the whole thing is a turn on. What do you think Mike?"

"I agree. Shall we get out of the car and watch?"

"Yes." We both get out of the car and walk across to where the action is happening. The lady seems to be getting egged on by the audience. She turns around so her arse is now on the front window and the old man is licking in between her legs. She starts to rub her boobs and pull all kinds of pleasure faces. Me and Penny hold hands, and Penny starts rubbing me over my jeans. We start kissing but I'm too intrigued in the live show we have before us, so I stop kissing her to look.

The car windows are getting really steamy, making it harder to see but now the couple is having sex. They have put the passenger seat back and the woman is lying down with the old man on top. We have more people around the car now, a lot of them are wanking furiously, then one by one they come and leave. Some of them drive away and some of them simply get back in their car and I suppose wait for the next show. The couple finishes their performance and put the seat back up. The old man gets back into the drivers seat, they do not acknowledge anyone; in fact they act like its a regular occurrence and drive off. Penny and I walk back to our car.

"Gosh that was hot."

"Yeah it was. What do we do now Mike?"

"I guess sit and wait for the next car."

We get back in the car and the young guy is still standing around, he is sort of heading our way. He probably thinks myself and Penny are going to do a show. I think about it for a minute, but I'm too excited to see what happens next.

A black BMW drives past us and the interior light goes on to reveal a good looking guy. For a moment I think it's Jude Law, but obviously it's not, but then saying that, you never know.

The car drives around for a bit. He's obviously showing off letting people know he's a good-looking guy. He comes back our way and flashes his lights three times. "What's he doing?" Penny asks.

"I don't know, wind down your window and ask the young guy," I tell Penny. She winds down the window. "Excuse me? Excuse me?"

He comes up to the window, and Penny says, "This is our first time. Why is that car flashing his lights at us?"

"That's because he wants you to join him. Follow him."

"Follow him where?"

"I don't know, another dogging spot."

"Ok, thanks."

Penny does up the window. "What do you think Mike?"

"I suppose it's ok, but anything dodgy we drive away."

We follow the car for about five minutes and pull off the road going down a little dirt track.

"I'm not sure about this Penny," I say.

Before our eyes we are in a camp field and there are about four cars, prestigious cars, elite cars: a Bentley, a Porsche, and a Mercedes. The guy in the BMW pulls up and we park next to him. Out of the Mercedes a hot chick, she must of been about 18, jumps out and gets into his car they greet each other with a kiss and pretty much start the action. The next minute all the interior lights of the cars go on to reveal couples getting it on. Our car is the only car that doesn't have the interior light on.

"Shall we do it Mike?"

"I don't know Pen, I'm liking being a voyeur. Why don't we get out of the car and watch?"

We get out of the car and Penny walks over to the black BMW whilst I walk over to the Bentley. Looking in the window, I get a big shock. It's a beautiful woman who looks like Cindy Crawford with lovely tits but a cock. A chick with a dick! I jump back.

"Penny! Watch this!"

Penny runs over. "OMG she has a dick!"

The young guy, he must be no older than 19, starts sucking on her/his whatever it is, cock, whilst holding her/his tits at the same time. Both me and Penny are gobsmacked. She is really beautiful -- everything about her is womanly until she opens her legs. She gets very hard then puts the guy on his back and starts having sex. Her/his boobs bounce up and down as he thrusts back and forth. Penny and I take the passengers window so we can see the face of the chick with a dick. She looks up at us and stares straight at us with 'come to bed eyes'. I start to feel a little uncomfortable and put my head down.

I then move to the Porsche where an older couple about 60ish are going at it. I watch for a little bit, but it's not one bit sexy, so I go back to the BMW where they are really going for it.

I hear noises and Penny is lying across the bonnet of the car playing with herself. She is so turned on that she makes herself come.

I continue to watch the BMW, but I feel stupid to get my cock out and wank. I think about opening the car door and joining in but I don't. Instead I go back to my car and wait for Penny to finish. Penny finishes and comes back to the car.

"How was that?" I ask.

"OMG that was so sexy. I came so hard. I really fancy that he/she and I would of loved to experience that. What about you?"

"Yeah, the same. I was very horny but I chickened out, and I'm desperate for the toilet. I didn't want to pull my cock out around here just in case they get the wrong idea."

We start the engine, put the headlights on and drive back up the dirt track. We stop and look behind us for one last look at the lights of the cars and their steamy windows, then drive off.

"That was something spectacular, don't you agree?"

"I sure do. I can't get the pictures out of my head. I don't think I'm ever going to get that picture out of my head," Penny says.

"Oh look Penny, there are some toilets. I have to go. Do you need to go?"

"No I don't. I will wait here, ok?"

I walk into the toilets and there are three cubicles. The cubicles are closed so I head straight for the urinals, "arh what a relief". Gosh I needed that. I pee so much then I hear a banging noise.

"Shit what's that?" – it's coming from the cubicles. I shout 'hello?'-- nobody answers me. I then hear groaning so I stop peeing and do up my zip and walk over to the cubicles.

The noise is coming from the middle one, so I look through the gap in the door and see a woman. She is doing something with her left hand, so I go to the urinal to the right and look through the gap. I see a man and there is a hole in the side of the divide he has his cock in it. I go back to the middle urinal and see that she is wanking his cock through the hole then I hear a come noise. The guy has come and the toilet door opens. The guy walks past me and out of the toilets, so I go into the cubicle and lock the door.

I look through the hole to see that her bum is touching the wall, and her pussy is facing me. The other guy in the other cubicle is obviously fucking her now. I can't see her face as the hole is cock height and the guy is banging the girl really hard. She is screaming and moaning with so much delight that I am getting so turned on.

I put my dick into the hole it just stays there for a while, my hard dick in a hole that has been made in a cubicle toilet. It's throbbing and hard, all I want her to do is touch it but she doesn't. I feel so stupid. I slowly take my hard cock out of the hole, but before I pull my cock out of the hole she grabs it and pulls it back through.

She then starts sucking it. I push my body flat to the partition so I can enable my cock to go through the hole the full length so she can go deep onto it. I want her mouth to go the full length; I want her mouth to go deep down onto it. She is sucking it really good my whole body starts to shake. I hear the other cubicle door open but I don't care who is watching. I don't think about Penny as I am so involved in what is happening to my cock.

She stops sucking it, then I feel something wet and spongy on the end of it. I pull away and kneel down to look through the hole and she has put her pussy up to it. I lick my finger a couple of times then I put it inside her and finger her vigorously. She moans and groans and pushes herself back onto my finger so I nest another one. She is getting wetter so I start wanking my cock with my free hand. Without thinking, I pull my fingers from out of her and stick my cock in, bang her hard, really hard. At one point my cock slips out of her and catches the side of the hole, which is kind of rough. I put my cock back inside of her and really fuck her. She is screaming and I'm banging my hands on the partition. As I'm about to climax, I come with a primal scream. I'm not sure if I pulled out in time but I pull my cock back through the hole, wipe myself with a tissue and leave the cubicle. When I leave there are three people waiting outside to enter.

       I jump back in the car and Penny is asleep. I do not wake her I just drive back to London thinking all the way about what a night we have had, but most of all my toilet experience. Will I tell Penny? Shit! I cannot believe I did that and enjoyed it. The evening plays over and over in my head. We reach the hotel. "Penny, we are here." She gets out of the car without saying a word, and does not even say a word in the lift. She jumps straight into bed and by the time I get in she is fast asleep.

Chapter Sixteen

"Good morning Penny."

"Morning."

"How do you feel?"

"Why?" She says defensively.

"No reason. It's just that you were a little tipsy. You polished off two bottles of wine by yourself."

"Oh well, I feel fine."

"So what do you fancy doing today, as we will have to back to Amsterdam tomorrow."

"I'm not sure," Penny says in a very aloof voice.

"Penny, are you ok?" I ask.

"Yeah. Why wouldn't I be?"

"I don't know. You seem like you're off with me. Have I done something to upset you?"

"Let me see," she says. "Do you think you have done anything?"

"Well actually, Penny, there is something I want to tell you. But whilst you're in this foul mood I will wait."

"No. Tell me. I want to know."

"Well last night when I stopped to use the toilets, I didn't just use the loo. I sort of fucked someone."

"I know."

"You do? How?"

"I walked into the toilets, as you were taking a long time. I couldn't see you but could hear noises. So I looked through the gap in the door and saw you… I saw you fucking. And there was nothing 'sort of' about it. You were fucking."

"I'm sorry Penny. I just got so turned on by the events that took place, and I couldn't join you

whilst you were pleasuring yourself on the car. I
don't know why, I just couldn't. So when I got to the
toilet and saw that it was something out of this world,
something so naughty, I wasn't myself. I wasn't
thinking. My dick was so hard that I didn't care. The
thought of getting caught made me harder, and the
thought of fucking a stranger was an even bigger turn
on. I'm so sorry."

"It's fine Mikey. I was upset because *one*, I
thought you were not going to tell me. I thought you
were going to lie to me."

"No Penny. I would never lie to you. Why
would I? I don't need to lie to you. I was always going
to tell you."

"I know you were. Thank you. *Two*, I am
upset by the fact that you didn't get me. Why didn't
you come and get me?"

"I don't know. It all happened so fast."

"This is *our* journey. We are supposed to be
on a journey *together*, and watching you made me feel
like I was not a part of it. It didn't feel good."

I grab Penny. "Look at me. I'm so sorry! This
will never happen again. I will never, ever do
anything with out you, I promise. Now can you stop
being angry and give me a kiss."

We have a kiss and then I ask Penny, "Come
on what do you want to do today? Anything you
want."

"Well I read about Harrods, can we go
there?"

"Yes of course."

"Also, let's try and go to that house of ill
repute, it sounds fun."

"Where was it?" I ask.

"The news said he was found coming out of a
place called Home House."

"Home House," I say, "Home House is a private members club. It can't be that place Penny; you must have the wrong details. I actually know a bar man there I will give him a ring."

"Hello Stephen, it's Mikey Taylor."

"Hi Mikey, long time. What do I owe the pleasure of this call?"

"Oh nothing important, mate. It's just I live abroad now and just got back. I overheard someone talking about an MP and a house and shenanigans that went on."

"Ah yes, *that*. Well, we now rent the house out to private promoters who put on their own events. This particular promoter was not forthcoming about the event he was doing in the house. He just told us that it was a high society party, beautiful girls and rich old men. He forgot to mention the fact that the men were elite and the girls were hookers. The press has had a field day on this story, it was not good for him, but good for us. Our bookings have gone up. In fact, we have another sexy masquerade party tonight. This time the credentials have been checked out and it's a genuine one. It should be a lot of fun."

"Yeah it sounds good. So how do I get an invite?"

"I will put your name down mate, no worries. Only requirement is masks before 11 pm. It starts at seven; no wearing masks, no entry. Oh and it's costume. That's what it says on the flyer I'm reading, so be sure to be in a costume and a mask."

"Thanks Stephen. Are you working tonight?"

"I'm not, I'm afraid. See you next time mate. Enjoy your evening."

So I tell Penny the news that we are going to a masquerade ball. "That's fantastic," she says. "I think we should go to Harrods quickly then go and get our masks and costumes and then get ready."

"Great idea."

We go to Harrods and practically buy the whole store. Penny is so excited by all the jams, marmalades and things that have the Queen pictured on it.

"I want a photo of us outside," Penny says. "Come on Mikey."

We go outside and get a picture of us holding up our Harrods bag.

"Ok," I say, "time to get our costumes. There's a costume shop about a 10 minute walk from here."

We start walking towards Green Park. "Mike can I ask you something?"

"Of course."

"Have you got a sexual fantasy?"

"No I don't think so."

"Come on, you must."

"That's a good question. I'm going to have to think about that. What about you?" If you had one sexual fantasy that you could act out what would it be?"

"The forced upon fantasy," Penny says.

"The what? What does that mean?"

"The rape fantasy," Penny explains.

"It sounds a little heavy and fucked up to me Penny."

"No it's not. A lot of women have this fantasy. I don't mean forced upon in a brutal way, being smacked around. I just mean it as the element of surprise. Just the not knowing when it's coming and how."

"Ok Penny." I change the subject, "Look here is the shop."

We enter to be greeted by a man in a Sherlock Holmes costume.

"Good afternoon, welcome," he says in an English Oxford University accent. "How can I help you both?"

"We are looking for costumes that we can wear to a masquerade ball."

"Excellent," he says. "I have the perfect costume for you," and points to Penny. "Your name dear?"

"Oh it's Penny."

"We have just gotten an original Marie Antoinette dress with all the accessories. The owner of the shop bid for it at an auction. It was very expensive. It will cost three thousand pounds for one night's hire." He shows us the dress. It is everything you could imagine and more.

"Wow Penny that would look amazing on you. Do you want it? Actually I insist you have it."

"And for you…?"

"Mike, my name is Mike."

"Okay Mike. For you a banyan, a pair of breeches, a coat, a cravat and a hat. Yes that will do," he says as he stands with one hand on his hip and the other hand on the pipe he is puffing on. "You both will look like the perfect 18th-century couple."

He wasn't lying. It was like stepping back in time.

"Now all we need are our masks." Penny picks an amazing white swan mask and I go for the plain black Zorro-looking mask. We go to the counter to pay and rush back to the hotel to get ready.

Penny comes out of the bathroom and looks amazing. Very Marie Antoinette.

"Penny?"

"Yes Mike?"

"All I can say is 'wow.'"

"Thank you, you look good too. I like your pants."

"You mean breeches."

"Yes you look very dapper. Mike, I have an idea. Let's do my fantasy. Come on, it will be fun. Come on let's have a real different experience. Let's go to the ball separately, let's not acknowledge each other at all, and then I want you to take me. Force me to have sex with you.   I want you to force yourself onto me."

"Oh I don't know about that Penny, and besides it might not be that type of party, it might just be a costume party."

"Well we will see." With that Penny leaves the hotel room.

I follow behind, but cannot see Penny. I go to the front desk. They tell me she just jumped into a black cab. So I ask them if they could also get me a taxi that will take me to Home House.

I arrive at Home House and a man opens my car door welcoming me to the masquerade ball. As I walk in the house I'm greeted with a glass of champagne.

The house is an actual eighteenth-century house -- the decor inside has not changed one bit. From the wallpaper on the walls, to the furniture, even down to the wooden poster beds that have so much detail engraved into the wood. The house also has the original copper bathtubs.   The main attraction of the house is the winding stairs that leads to the rooms.   At the top of the staircase is a pretty impressive chandelier.

I look around, and the party already seems to be in full swing. A lot of people obviously have had the same idea as Penny and myself with regards to costumes – there are a lot of Marie Antoinette outfits. The promoter has not skimped on this party at all, every attention to detail, down to the music and the low lighting.

I walk up the stairs and enter the ballroom, lots of couples all masked and not one face to be seen. They are all doing a traditional 18th-century dance.

I walk out of that room and go into the piano room. There are about three Marie Antoinette's listening to a guy that is wearing, I guess, a costume from *Wuthering Heights*. I think he is trying to be Heathcliff.

Then I walk into one of the bedrooms, with a load of pillows and cushions are on the floor. A lady is in the tub; she is fully naked apart from her huge beehive wig. Four couples enter the room all kissing, laughing, and joking. They get down onto the cushions on the floor and start having sex. I leave this room and enter another ballroom.

This room is really crowded with a lot of people dancing. There are a lot more Marie Antoinette's. How am I ever going to find Penny? Everyone looks the same, and I can't remember all the details of her dress. I didn't see her in her mask; I only know that it is a white swan mask. There are at least five girls in this room wearing the same as Penny.

I walk back out of that room, and walk down a corridor. A little way ahead of me I see Penny, well I think it's Penny, so I speed up until I'm really close to her back. From behind I'm not sure if it is Penny, as it could be another Marie Antoinette. "Excuse me," I say.

She turns around; she is wearing a swan mask. I grab her left arm and look at it. Penny has a little star tattoo on the inside of her wrist. Yes it's Penny, as she has the tattoo. I pull her really hard. She says, "What are you doing?"

"Come with me," I say as I pull her into a bathroom toilet.

I push her into the toilet -- it's very small, hardly enough room for both of us, with just a toilet and a sink. I grab her throat. She chokes a little.

"I can't breathe," she says.

I let my grip around her throat go. I tell her to turn around, she does. I can't take her costume off, as it's so big, so I just lift up the dress and rip off her knickers. "Ow," she says, "Ow."

I say, "I will give you ow." I bend her over the toilet and I push her head down so it touches the top of the cistern, then I get my dick out and fuck her hard.

"No," she says. "No!"

"Come on you little slut, you love it." I keep fucking her, her head is bouncing of the top of the toilet, the cistern. She actually starts to moan in delight and her pussy gets really wet, then I come. I don't come inside her; I pull out and come all over her arse. I then leave the toilet cubicle, go back downstairs and get a drink.

Eleven o'clock strikes on the big old grandfather clock, and everyone removes their masks. Ah that's better, I can see now. Where is Penny? I look around, in fact, I look in all of the rooms even the toilet, the last place I had seen her but she was not there. Maybe she has gone back to the hotel? I leave the house and head back for the hotel.

153

I get in the room and there is still no sign of Penny. Strange. I grab my mobile to call her, but then I hear a key card in the door. I open the door and in falls a very drunk Penny.

"Mikey, there you are. I have been looking all over for you! What a fun party, as you can see I am very drunk."

"I can see that. I was looking for you too for ages. Where did you disappear after our toilet scene and did you enjoy it? Did I fulfill your fantasy for you?"

"What are you talking about Mike? What toilet? I didn't go to the toilet once. I was out in the garden all night drinking with some," as she hiccups, "fabulous people."

"No Penny. I did the forced fantasy on you."

"I wish you did! I was waiting all night for the element of surprise. I thought you must have fallen asleep in the hotel that's why you didn't show up. That's why I'm back." With that she passes out on the bed.

Surely Penny is not that drunk that she can't remember me fucking her in the toilet! She will remember in the morning, I bet. I try and reassure myself that it is Penny. I have a glimpse at her arm, yes the same tattoo on her wrist, and her body and pussy felt like Penny, it must have been Penny. Who else could it of been? She is just drunk and playing with me, she will remember in the morning.

"Good morning my drunken little skunk."

"Oh God! I feel awful," she says as she buries herself under the covers. "I never want to drink again in my life."

"Yeah that's what you're saying now."

"My head hurts," Penny says. "I need some aspirin."

"So, has your memory come back?"

"Yeah. Sort of… I think actually I do. I remember I had so much fun. Well obviously I did, as my head is pounding. Thank you Mike, it was a great evening. You did a great job."

"Thank God you remembered. You had me worried all night that I couldn't sleep. I knew you would remember."

The phone rings, and it is Greg. "Hey Mike, the twins will be at your office at two."

"What? I'm in London."

"Well get yourself back on a plane. The gold deal is doing really well and they want to invest more money. Where are you?"

"I'm at the Marriott hotel around the corner from my house."

"What are you doing there?"

"It's a long story, Greg."

"Ok well, I will get a driver and I will get you a flight on the next plane."

"Oh Greg, you will also need to get a ticket for a Ms. Penny Snow."

"Who?"

"Like I said it's a long story."

"Ok whatever you say."

"Come on Penny, get showered and dressed. We have to leave ASAP. I need to be back in Amsterdam."

With a huge hangover voice and still under the covers, Penny asks, "What about taking the costumes back?"

"Don't worry about them, I will get the hotel to organize their return."

Chapter Seventeen

We arrive at London Heathrow airport we have an hour and a half before our plane boards.

"I'm in need of some food," Penny says.

"And by the look of you, I say you could do with some hair of the dog. Come on let's sort out my delicate sugar tits. So what do you fancy eating?"

"Oh I don't know, salmon and eggs, eggs and something, and I think a Bloody Mary as well."

"That will definitely cure your hangover."

We find a quiet Irish pub and order Penny's food. She struggles to eat her food, but manages to drink her drink in one go. As soon as her Bloody Mary is finished all the colour comes back to her face.

"You know, yesterday, when I told you about my fantasy, I wasn't actually being 100 percent honest. That wasn't my ultimate fantasy."

"You're winding me up, right Penny?"

"No I'm not."

"So go on. Tell me, what is your ultimate fantasy."

"No it doesn't matter because you won't do it anyway."

"Lie about it?"

"It is a very big fantasy and a very big ask."

"Well, why don't you tell me and I can decide for myself. As long as it's not seeing another bloody dominatrix again, that's something I'm not doing."

"No, it's not that. You know that night when we were in the countryside at the dogging site? Well I can't get that woman/he/she out of my head. It really turned me on."

"Well that's not a problem, I'm sure we can find plenty of chicks with dicks in Amsterdam. The Red Light is full of them."

"No, that's not it. It's not the thought of the woman with a dick that's turning me on. It's the thought of a man, dressed as a woman, that is doing it for me."

"Ok Penny. Yes that is a little too much. I'm not sure about that."

"Oh come on Mike, be a sport."

"I have been a sport. I've been a sport since the day I met you."

"And haven't you had fun? Hasn't the sex journey been out of this world?"

"Out of this world for sure."

"Oh please, Mikey. It is the ultimate fantasy for me. I promise you if you help me with this fantasy, I will do whatever you want. I will do your ultimate fantasy, whatever it is for 24 hours, I promise. Come on. I'd be your bitch for you to do whatever you like for 24 hours."

"24 hours you say?"

"Yep 24 hours."

With a lot more persuading and those big sexy blue eyes staring at me, I say, "Ok you're on. So what are you suggesting?"

"I would love it if I could feminize you."

"Did I just hear you right? No way in a million years! I'm not being a fucking woman! It's gay and I'm not gay."

"No it's not gay, it's just a fantasy."

"Well maybe this fantasy is just best left in your head Penny. Come on choose another one. I will do anything else, even the Dom or butt plug thing again."

"No Mike, that's what I want."

"Ok, ok, you win." I'm telling you something strange has happened to both Penny and I since the toilet fun. I'm obsessing about dogging thing and

Penny now wants to do ultimate fantasy sex. I wonder if dogging happens in Amsterdam? Maybe that could be my next book, *A Fortnight of Dogging*?

"British Airways flight 428 is now boarding. Could all passengers please proceed to the gate."

"Come on my little fantasist," I laugh to myself, "We have to board the plane."

We get on the plane, and again I have a look at the views outside the window as the plane takes off, and believe it or not a sigh of relief comes over me. I'm not sad to be leaving London I'm actually happy about going back to Amsterdam.

"Hello Dick"

"Hi Mr. Taylor."

"How was your flight?"

"Short but sweet, always a pleasant flight. And how have you been Dick?"

"I've been very well, thank you. A lady friend of mine came to visit me whilst you were away. I just dropped her to the train before I picked you up. "

"Oh good I'm glad you had a nice time. Could you drop me of at the office first please Dick, then take Penny back to the apartment. This sleepy girl needs a sleep. She had too much to drink last night, Dick."

"Ok Penny wake up we're here at my office. I have a meeting for a couple of hours then I will be straight back."

"Ok," she says, in a very sleepy voice. I give her a kiss and Dick drives off. I feel great this morning. I'm going to walk the stairs again.

"Good morning Amelia, please could you get the meeting room ready. We have a very important meeting today."

"No problem Mike."

The twins actually turned up two hours early for the meeting, which was fantastic, which meant I could go home early and spend some quality time snuggled up to my sugar tits. Yeah right, Penny had a different plan for me.

"Hello my lovely I'm home. How was your day?"

"So far good, I slept a little more. Had an omelet then I have spent the last couple of hours researching on the Internet."

"Researching what?"

"My ultimate fantasy," she says.

"Oh that. I thought I was let off the hook."

"No way."

"Okay."

"So tell me what does feminization mean?"

"It means that I'm going to make you into a woman, and you will have to also get into character and act like one. Now if you're not going to have an open mind and get into it and into character, then let's not do it," Penny says. "I want this to be so real after all it is my fantasy and you will get to do yours for a whole 24 hours."

"Ok Penny, fine. I will give it 100 percent. So what's the first thing we are doing?"

"We are going shopping, but before we go shopping we have to start the feminization process. In order for this to work you must start walking like a girl."

"How the hell do I do that?"

"Well that's easy. I want you to walk up and down swinging your hips from side to side." I get up

159

and start walking up and down the living room. I laugh, "Penny I feel stupid."

"Nuh uh, remember you have to take it seriously, oh and you need a girl's name. I need to start calling you by your girl's name."

"And what's that going to be?"

"I think Melissa, yep Melissa, that suits you. So carry on walking Melissa. Try putting your hands on your hips like so and really move those hips from side to side."

Penny gets up and grabs my hips and starts pushing them from side to side. "That's it," she says, "you're doing a great job Melissa."

"Now practice your girl voice, as your voice is too low at the moment. Why don't we start with just the alphabet, come on Melissa."

In a slow girl's voice I start to say "a-b-c-d."

"No," Penny says. "Stop. It's too low. Listen to me, listen to my voice," she says. "Come on, concentrate."

So I listen to Penny then I correct myself. "How does this sound?" I say "a-b-c-d."

"Wonderful that sounds great."

"Oh I need the toilet," I still say in my girls voice, as I walk into the toilet unzip my jeans, and go to pull my dick out.

Penny come barging in. "No what are you doing? You mustn't stand up peeing. Girls don't stand they sit," she says.

"Oh yes I'm sorry," I say in my newfound high-pitch voice. I sit down to pee. It takes a while as I'm used to peeing standing up, but it finally comes, then I get the tissue, wipe myself and stand up.

"Did you wash your hands," Penny shouts.

160

"Well of course I did."

"Right now we have got the Melissa walk and talk, so its time to go shopping. Can you call Dick? We will need a ride and you must still speak to him in your girl voice."

"No way Penny."

"Yes way. 24 hours remember you will get your turn."

I clear my voice, hem hem. "Hello Dick."

"Yes Mike, what's wrong with your voice," he asks.

"Oh nothing I have a bit of a cold. Well actually Penny and me have a bet, and I have to speak like this for 24 hours. Can you please take us to a shop? It's called Suddenly Fem, and it's a cross dressing shop, Dick."

"Ok," as he laughs.

"It's not a laughing matter, so please don't laugh. I have to take it seriously."

"I'm sorry," still chuckling, "I will be with you in five minutes."

"Thank you," I say, still in my girl's voice.

Dick arrives and all the way to the car I do not say a word, as I feel embarrassed. It's one thing for Dick to hear me like this on the phone but to hear it in person is a no.

We arrive at the shop; it's a small shop. We go in to be greeted by an older lady who is reading a newspaper behind the till.

"Goedemorgen," she says, and both Penny and I nod. She then gets back to reading her paper.

"Penny," I whisper still in my girl voice, "is that a man or woman?"

"I don't know," she replies.

Penny says we will start with the makeup section. "We will need beard shadow, cover that will hide the marks of your beard after you are clean shaven, then we will need to get the foundation. I think you are a medium. Let me just try a bit," so she gets a tiny bit and puts it onto my chin. "Yep that's your colour," so we put this into the basket.

"We will need eye shadow, eyeliner, mascara, lip liner and lipstick, bronzer and blusher." Penny gets all the testers and starts putting them on me to see if the colour is nice. I just stand there letting her do it to me, while the woman at the front desk is still reading the paper.

"Next we need eyelashes, I think we will get the individual ones rather than the strips," she says. This is over my head I have no clue what she's talking about so I just smile.

"I think that's all the makeup we need, now let's go and get you some boobs. What size boobs would you like," Penny asks.

"Well if I'm going to have boobs," I say, "I want the biggest pair."

So we go to the boob section and there are loads of different sizes with different size nipples. They even have flesh type nipples and brown nipples. The ones I like the look of are the new perky breasts with clear straps. They look so natural, size DD and are molded into a stretchy clear, lucite bra so I pick them up. "Wow Penny! Feel these, they feel so real."

Both Penny and myself stand there for a minute squeezing them and molding them into our hands. "If we're getting you boobs we may as well get you a pussy as well."

"A pussy?" I say.

162

Penny pulls out a lifelike looking vagina, it looks so real. "It reminds me of the Fleshlight," I say. "So how does this work?"

"You step into it like a G-string. You insert the penis inside the sheath which will allow both of us to experience sexual pleasure." In my head I'm thinking no way this is too freaky. I don't tell Penny this, I just agree in my girl's voice.

"Ok shoes." She asks, "What shoes do you like?"

"I don't know, they all look good," I say.

"Well why don't we try a few pairs on?"

I look around to make sure no one is looking, and still the woman or man from behind the till is reading; and there is no one in the shop apart from us. So we get a red pair, black pair, and silver pair. I try them all on and walk up and down the store. The most comfortable pair and the pair I could still walk with were the silver stripper looking pair that have a stiletto heel only 3 inches. It has a clear plastic front that your feet just mold into.

"Now we need your clothes. I think you should wear a black corset, black knickers, fishnet hold ups, and long, black leather gloves." We pick my size and put them into the basket.

"What's missing?" Penny muses as her eyes scan the basket.

I mutter, "How am I supposed to know?"

"Did I just hear a man's voice?" Penny asks.

"No," I say. I look around still no one is looking. I feel really stupid and embarrassed, like I'm a child that has been told off. I don't think I can go through with this, as this is humiliating. I pull Penny aside. "Penny, I feel stupid and humiliated. Is this some stupid game of yours or is this for real?"

"No it's for real. She says, "It's my genuine fantasy of a lifetime. I've dreamt of this for three years."

I look at her, give a kiss, and say in my girl's voice, "Nails what about false nails?" If it's Penny's fantasy then I'm going to get into it, and get something out of it as well.

"Jewelry." I also say, "and of course Melissa wouldn't be complete without a wig. Come along Penny let's get Melissa a wig. Do you thing Melissa is a blonde, brunette or redhead, long hair or medium length?"

We grab three wigs. I try them on and we both agree that Melissa is definitely a long-haired blonde with a fringe. "Come along Penny, I think we have everything now."

"Excuse me this is my fantasy. We are not done, we need a strap-on otherwise you can't fuck me."

"I have a dick."

"Oh no you don't. You now have a pussy, it's in the basket."

"Oh yeah, I forgot."

"So let's get this one." Penny says, "it's got a rippled shaft 6 inch long and one and a half inch wide. That will do nicely."

We go to the checkout and the woman behind the till says "good choice of boobs. They are very comfy. I've got the exact pair on now."

"Why thank you," I say, and walk out the shop.

We get back into the car, Dick asks "where to now?" Still in my girl's voice, I reply, "Home please Dick."

Back at the apartment we empty the bag of our purchases and line them all up. Penny runs a bath. "Melissa we need to get a bath, come on." We both go into the bathroom and Penny starts washing me.

"Ok I'm going to immac your legs, arms, underarms, genital area and your legs." I ask why. "Because girls don't have hair."

She says, "First I have to shave you, as your hair is too long." She gets conditioner and tells me to sit on the side of the bath. She gets the razor puts the conditioner into my pubes, this will make them nice and soft and easy to shave, and starts shaving my dick and my balls. I actually start to get hard. Penny pays no attention to my hardness and carries on shaving. She tells me to bend over, as she has to shave my bum. I feel a little nervous as razors are sharp and she could cut me. I close my eyes and think about football until it's over. She then shaves my armpits, and then makes me stand up. She gets the immac and puts it all over my body; instantly it starts to sting. "Ouch Penny it's stinging."

"Well it has to stay on for six minutes to get all the hair off. Why don't you shave your face? Make sure every bit of hair is off, as we want good coverage on the makeup and it will take your mind off the immac."

I shave my face, making sure to take every bit of hair off; I look 10 years younger. Penny says its time for the immac to come off. She gets a sponge, puts some soap on and starts rubbing my skin. All my hair does come off then she gets the shower attachment and showers me down. "Look at yourself."

I look into the mirror. "Wow all my hair is gone. It looks really strange, it doesn't look like my body, it even feels different; it feels soft." Penny then smothers my whole body in moisturizing cream.

"Time for the makeup."

She gets a cotton ball and wipes my face with a toner. "Ouch that stings as well. What was that?"

"Oh it's alcohol based," she says. "I'm stripping your skin. Stopping the oils so the makeup will stay on." She puts the beard cover up on followed by the foundation, then the eye shadow.

"I'm going to do a smoky look," she says. "A smoky look is really sexy. How are you feeling?"

"Great," I say. The truth is, it actually did. It felt nice to be pampered. It was pampering in a different way. The makeup felt alien at first, it was cold and felt heavy on my skin, but after a while I couldn't feel it. The eyelashes were the strangest feeling in the world. My eyes felt heavy and at one point the glue that was used to put them on stuck my bottom eyelid to the top eyelid. The lipstick smelt and tasted really good, so good that I kept licking it off. Penny had to apply it three times before it stayed on.

Penny put the boobs on me next, they also felt heavy and the strap was tight on my back but from the front they felt amazing. They felt like the real thing. I cupped both of them in my hands and moved them up and down, and then I tweaked the nipples a little.

Penny then put on the pussy. My dick was starting to get hard. I don't know if it was because the boobs, or the fact that Penny was fiddling down there was turning me on. "Mike I can't put it on if your cock is hard."

"Well maybe I should put it on so you're not playing with it," I say. Penny turns around and I put the pussy over my dick. "There, it's done," I say.

Penny turns back around. "Now we will have to get you dressed. Hold the corset onto your boobs." I hold it while Penny starts doing it up from behind. "Jesus that's tight Penny."

"It has to be tight, that's what a corset is."

"I can't breathe."

"Yes you can, your body will adapt to it soon."

"I hope so." Penny helps me to get into the panties and tells me to sit on the toilet seat and lift one leg so she can put the fishnet hold ups on. "These feel good," I say. The fishnet against my skin feels really sexy. "It's a different feeling to wearing jeans or trousers."

"Your legs look great in them," Penny says admiringly. "You have got good legs."

Next we put on the wig and the clip on jewelry --diamanté dangling earrings and a diamanté-matching necklace.

Penny says, "Let's put the false nails on." She gets them out of the pack, matches them up to my own nails and puts the glue on to my fingernails. "How will I get them off?"

"Good question," Penny says. "I'm sure we can just soak your hands in acetone, that's what you use to take of nail varnish. Speaking about nail varnish, your nails would look great coloured pink." So she grabs a nail varnish and starts painting my nails.

"There you go, nice pink nails. Wave them around for a bit as they're wet and need to dry." I wave my hands then blow on them. "I think you have to have matching toes," so Penny then paints my toenails. "Last it is time to put on the wig." Penny puts the wig on and tells me it's time to look in the mirror.

"I can't," I say. "I feel scared."

"Don't be scared Melissa, you look beautiful. Close your eyes," she says and guides me to the mirror. "After three open them. One, two, three," and I open my eyes. I jump back from the mirror.

"Is that really me? Oh my God I look totally different. I do look like a girl. A total transformation."

I'm shocked! I'm so shocked. I never thought I would look this good. I've seen men in drag before, but this doesn't look like I'm a man in a dress. I actually look convincing, well at least I think I do.

"So now what?" I say to Penny.

"Well I think you should put your shoes on." I put on the shoes, but I'm still wobbly.

"Why don't you walk around a bit to get used to the shoes?" I walk up and down and can't help looking at myself in the mirror. I have actually forgotten that I'm Mike, and really get into my character. I'm Melissa.

"So what are us girlies going to do now?"

"I think we should put some music on and drink some wine." We drink some wine; well I literally down a whole bottle. Penny then says, "let's dance."

She puts on a slow song and we dance really slowly. Penny's arms are around my neck, she looks straight into my eyes.

"Mellissa," she says, "you're so pretty. I really fancy you. Would you mind if I kissed you?"

"No," I say in a quiet voice.

She smells my lips and then kisses my lips softly. I can taste my lipstick on her lips and wow it tastes good. She then moves her hands through my long wig and down to my back and then my bum. She brings her hands to the front of me and starts rubbing my boobs. Obviously I can't feel it, but I can imagine what it feels like. She asks me to lie down so I lie on

168

the floor and close my eyes. Penny just runs her fingers delicately over my face, and rubbing one finger around my lips, she kisses them again. I just lie there and let her take control. I let her do all the pleasuring.

She then runs her fingers down to the corset and undoes one button at a time to reveal the big DD boobs. Her hands are cupping them. Again I open my eyes and look at Penny, she is fascinated with my boobs. She holds them both then she cups the left breast in both hands, smells it, and starts kissing it. She starts licking the nipple whilst tweaking the other nipple with the other hand. She moves over to the right breast and licks the nipple of that breast and then tweaks the other nipple. She then licks in between my boobs and dribbles her tongue all the way to my belly button and starts kissing my belly button.

She slowly brings her tongue down to my cock area. I'm so hard, my cock is throbbing but because of the pussy it's trapped. I was hoping it would poke through the opening of the pussy but it does not, only the helmet does. Penny gently kisses the clit on the pussy, I can't feel it but it looks good. Penny is certainly enjoying it, she is moaning then she gets her tongue and puts it in the opening of the pussy, which actually touches my helmet. She stays there for a while and it feels good. Still licking, her hands reach up to my boobs. She then stops licking me and asks me to undress her.

"Undress me Melissa," she says.

I tell her, "Lets go into the bedroom."

We go into the bedroom and I stand her in front of the mirror. I stand behind her so she can see my face. I put my hands to her breasts; she puts her hands over the top making sure she can see the nail varnish. She then guides my hands down her body. I start kissing her neck; I look into the mirror to see all my lipstick is over my face and on Penny's face and neck. I kiss her neck passionately with soft bites. Penny moans as she pushes my hands further down her body until I push her skirt down.

I then kneel down in front of Penny she still is facing the mirror so she can see my bare arse and my long hair touching my back. I kiss the top of her bikini line, smelling it each time I kiss it. Then I move down to her clitoris and tell her to open her legs. As I lick her clit, her legs start to shake. I stand back up and kiss her on the lips.

She tells me she wants to fuck me and gets the strap-on and puts it on me. She then gets a chair and makes me sit down on the chair. She sucks the strap-on and then straddles me. She holds on to my boobs whilst she jumps up and down then she kisses me again.

"Your lipstick has come off, you need more lipstick." She goes and gets the lipstick puts it on herself then puts it on me. We kiss and her lipstick goes all over my face and my lipstick on her face. She then tells me to fuck her. Penny goes down to the floor in doggy style position. I enter her pussy and start to thrust the plastic cock in and out of her. The inside of the strap-on is rubbing on my helmet, which is making me very horny. I look at Penny's face in the mirror she is just watching my boobs bounce up and down. I look at them too it looks very horny and realistic.

"Fuck me harder Melissa, let me feel all of you inside of me." I push the plastic cock deep inside her then pull it out slowly. I just put the tip on and tease her with it until she begs, "Please Melissa fuck me."

170

I do it three or four times she goes to rub her clit but I stop her from touching it. I roll her onto her back; lift her legs up high so they're on my shoulders then I thrust deep inside her. "Let me touch your tits!" She cries out, "Let me squeeze those big, bouncy tits!" I move her legs off my shoulders so she can reach the boobs. She cups them so tightly as I fuck her hard, really hard. She leaves one hand on my boob and plays with her clitoris as she gets wetter she starts to scream really loud, "Melissa, Melissa! I'm coming! I'm coming!" She comes and lets out a big sigh. I then lie on top of her and kiss her some more. I ask, "So how did I do?"

"That was perfect," she says. "That was so amazing you have no idea. Thank you for helping me with my fantasy it was truly one amazing experience."

"I'm glad I could oblige. Did I play the part right? Was I girly enough for you?"

"Yes you were," she says.

"Can I be Michael now? Can I use Michael's voice?"

"Yes of course," she says. "How did you feel being Melissa?"

"I have to say Penny, at first I was not convinced. I didn't think I would get into it, but the moment you put the makeup on me it changed the way I was feeling. Mike started dissolving and the more you feminized me the more Melissa was coming out. I do have to say I don't want to make a habit of this fantasy, and I'm not opposed to trying it again, especially because you forgot Melissa's gloves. I'm only joking. Is it possible to take this bloody wig off? I'm boiling hot under here."

"Yes you can take it off." I take the wig off and my hair is soaking wet. "Penny I'm going to have to jump in the shower again. What shall I take this makeup off with?"

"You can use the face scrub that is in the shower, but before you do let me take off those eyelashes." She pulls at my eyelashes. "Ow it hurts!"

"Don't be a baby," she says. "It doesn't hurt." With that she pulls them off.

"Now let's take off the nails." We soak then in a bowl of acetone but they do not move. "Shit Penny they're not coming off."

Penny laughs at me. "Why are you laughing? It's not funny."

"It is," she says.

"Well I'm glad you find it funny as I do not." The only thing that is coming off is the nail varnish. "I have an idea," she says. She goes and collects some nail clippers and cuts the nails as far as they will go.

"Great! A nail on top of a bloody nail."

"Well nobody will be able to see that you have false nails on," she says.

I huff then get in the shower. I jump out of the shower and I still have make up under my eyes. "Penny I look like a bloody panda." She comes into the bathroom with some cotton wool and some makeup remover.

"Come let me take the rest off." She gently wipes away the roaming makeup from under my eyes. I go into the bedroom to put some comfy track pants on and Penny clears up the apartment of all our fantasy bits.

Chapter Eighteen

I'm sitting comfortably in the living room when Penny asks me, "So mister, have you thought about your ultimate fantasy?"

"Good question," I say. "I have not. I don't know where to begin."

"Just let your mind wander," Penny says, "It will come to you. Remember you have me for a full 24 hours to do as you wish with me. I'm off for a long soak in the bath, my body aches."

"Are you ok?" I ask Penny.

"Yes I'm fine." Penny goes to the bathroom and I sit there thinking about my ultimate fantasy. It's really hard to think that 13 days ago I was not in this situation and my life was very different too. Well sexually it was. All the things I have experienced in the last few weeks have been my ultimate fantasy at least I think so. I mean I have experienced a threesome. I have experienced anal sex. I have experienced swinging. I have experienced dogging. I have experienced a dominatrix. I've experienced sleeping with a hooker, although Penny is not one, but when I first met her she was. So what more is there left to do? I go into the bathroom.

"Surely Penny I have experienced most sexual fantasies haven't I?"

She says no. "What do you mean no?"

"What we have experienced is not even half of our journey. We have a long way to go, a lot more things to explore. I'm going to have to take more than two weeks off work."

"Bloody hell," I say. "Ok I will leave you to soak."

I go back to the living room. Gosh this is tricky, why can't I think of a fantasy? I close my eyes and try and think back to the nights when I could wank in my bed and not in the office. What did I think about? But nothing entered into my head apart from a recent thing that I have just experienced, which was the toilet. Gosh that was so sexy, I don't know if anything else could be that sexy. Could it?

I get my laptop and Google around to see if there is anything out there that resonates with me. One thing that pops up whilst doing a search was a nurse's outfit. That's an idea! I think to myself. Then a fetish party pops up, it says Rubber Dolly Fetish Night. That looks interesting, so I enter the site and read about it. They talk about BDSM, live stage shows, PVC Rubber and latex. Reading it I get turned on. I want to go there, it sounds good and it's tomorrow night. That's perfect, I think. I go back into the bathroom and tell Penny that tomorrow night we are going to a fetish party, and that today I want her to go and buy every sexy outfit she can find.

"Like what," she asks.

"Like a naughty nurse outfit, any role play outfits you can find, and you need an outfit for tomorrow night, the theme is rubber dolly.

"Oh I like the sound of that," she says and jumps out of the bath. "How exciting! I don't think we have done fantasy role play with costumes, have we?" "No," I say, but it's not my ultimate fantasy. We will get to that."

"Can you call Dick for me," Penny says, "and tell him I will be ready in five minutes?"

"Penny, Dick is here."

"I'm coming." She gives me a kiss on the lips and shuts the door.

I jump on the bed and daydream. I revisit in my mind each and every sexual experience that has happened over the last fortnight. I even revisit the

174

first night I met Penny and how she blew me away and still does. But out of everything, I just cannot get out of my head the dogging experience. Was it the toilet or was it the outside sex, maybe it was a bit of both. Who knows, but I liked it very much. I get the laptop and find dogging spots in Amsterdam. Outside of Amsterdam, to be exact, I also find a nudist beach, as well as swinging holidays and all sorts of kinky things.

Buzz buzz. I get up to answer the door. It's Penny.

"I'm sorry Mike, I forgot my key."

"That's ok," I say, "gosh you were quick."

"I know I only needed to go into one shop. Come on let me show you what I bought. Where shall we do the fashion show?"

"Lets do it in the living room, that way I can sit on the couch and you will have a lot of room."

First up is the sailor suit. Little blue hot pants with a red and white top and a white hat, it's very nice. Penny walks up and down then she starts posing, and I get my iPhone and start taking pictures of her.

"I have an idea let's do a photo shoot. Each outfit you get more and more dirtier and more of the outfit comes off." With the sailor outfit Penny reveals nothing, just a lot of sexy poses and I take a lot of sexy photos.

The next outfit is a very naughty military army suit. Actually it is a romper suit that has a zip that goes all the way up the suit from the crotch to the boobs, so you can pull the zip down seductively to reveal the body. The suit also has fishnet side cut outs, a matching hat, belt, and thigh gun holster. Penny looks very hot in this outfit. She starts by taking the hat off, and then she teases the camera and me with the zipper. She pulls it down very slowly to reveal the top of her breasts. She is getting turned on by the stripper type of poses and all the teasing she is doing. And I'm getting turned on by taking the photos and by the fact of how great she looks on camera.

Next Penny puts on a general punishment costume. Imagine a 1940s German women's uniform, only a sexy one with stockings and a cane. She marches into the room banging her cane on the floor, lifts her leg onto the table whilst putting the cane in between her teeth. She seductively undoes her suspenders and belt, then takes off her knickers, flashes her bum at me and then walks out.

Next she walks into the room wearing a very sexy French maids outfit with a feather duster and marigold yellow gloves. Very purvey. She poses with the duster and gloves suggestively, putting the gloves in her mouth, lifting up her maids skirt to dust her arse. She even comes over and dusts my cock. This outfit looks good on my iPhone; I can really imagine the role-play with this one. She slowly and seductively takes the whole outfit off, apart from the gloves. One glove covers her boob whilst the other covers her pussy.

The next suit is my favorite, it's the naughty nurses outfit that comes with accessories: a nurses bag, a nurse stethoscope, even a temperature thing to put under your tongue.

Penny walks in, asking, "so what's wrong with you today?"

She comes over to the sofa and puts the stethoscope on my chest. "Oh no," I say, "I'm not a patient. I'm actually the Doctor and you have been caught in the act. Is this what you do to the patients of this hospital Nurse?"

"I'm sorry Doctor I don't normally, it's just you are so good looking I couldn't resist."

"I don't believe you Nurse. We had a complaint last week because one of the patients thought it wasn't fair that he didn't get the same type of bed bath you gave another patient. Now if you want to keep your job here you have to convince Doctor."

With that she starts to undress, until she is fully naked. She then lies on the floor with her legs spread wide. "How is this Doctor? Is that convincing enough? Would Doctor like to taste?"

"Oh no but I will watch you play with yourself. Let me see how wet you can get yourself, you naughty Nurse." Penny proceeds to get herself off while I carry on taking pictures. "Did Nurse come?"

"Oh yes, Nurse did come. In fact, Nurse could use a little cock."

"Well I'm afraid I have to return back to my doctor duty, we will continue this Nurse another day. Now run along."

Penny leaves the room then comes out wearing the rubber dolly outfit.
It's actually a rubber college girl outfit, very kinky indeed. Penny also has her hair tied up in pigtails and her white PVC socks pulled up to her knees.

"Oh Penny, wow! What an outfit. You can't wear that now, you will spoil it for tomorrow night. Tomorrow is the fetish club."

"Oh spoilsport. I want to wear it now."

"I know you do, but I want to enjoy tomorrow, and besides it's my fantasy. So go on, take it off."

Reluctantly she agrees, "Okay. And besides, I'm very tired and could do with an early night."

With that, Penny takes the outfit off and I get ready for bed.

Chapter Nineteen

The next morning Penny woke up with the flu, so we didn't get to do my fantasy. She in fact, had that horrid flu for two weeks. And in the two weeks she was sick, a lot happened to me at work, and a lot happened with Kelly too. Six months have now passed and it's the first day of summer and Penny and I are off on a two-week vacation, that's right, *A Fortnight of Fun*.

So what has happened in the last six months, I hear you say. Gosh where do I start? Well, like I said, we didn't make it to the fetish club, that's still on our to do list. We haven't finished the porn film either, as we decided we would finish that on this trip.

Basically I would say that all good things have happened in the last six months. Remember the gold deal I was working on? Oh I didn't tell you about it.

I had this contact that came across a gold mine, a lot of gold. But him and his partner, the guy who owned the farm, they needed investment to buy the machines that extract and produce the gold. The Yang twins invested. My mate Ronny was the contact. To his and everyone's surprise it was producing more gold than they ever thought was imaginable. This meant they needed more manpower, which meant more investment. The twins invested more and still this day the gold is still producing vast amounts. Their initial investment was six million pounds and their return so far has been 24 million pounds. They have more to come. My portion was four million pounds. With that and the money I already had, I thought it was time to retire and enjoy my life, so I have spent the last six months setting up my new business.

I'm pleased to say it is now up and running. A part of our trip is to also find some exciting things for the business. The new business is Penny Snow online.com It is real, and if you type in www.pennysnowonline.com it will bring you to a fantastic website that has all your fantasy needs. Everything you need for a night of pleasure.

We sell perfumes and one in particular, *Pink Mafia*. I came up with the name after Penny told me her story about her dad and the mob. I thought it was funny. She saw the humor and kept the name of it. You know, I actually had that perfume especially made in France for Penny. She chose the scent; it's a sexy perfume that has something in it to turn you on. It's actually been sprayed on the pages of this book. We also sell Pink Mafia lingerie, stockings, body melting candles, toys for him and her, and erotic films. Once our film is finished it will be on the site. Erotic books including this one and lots more fun stuff, so check it out www.pennysnowonline.com.

Alongside the website shop we are also going to open a physical shop, Penny Snow Boutique. I'm still waiting for the lease of the property to be signed over. Not long now I hope.

Let's see, what else has been happening in the last 6 months? Oh yes, so when I retired there was no one to take over the Amsterdam office and Greg made Simon do it, as Greg's son wanted to join the firm. Which at first took some time to get my head around, as even though I sorted things out with Kelly I still had anger towards Simon.

Kelly started coming over most weekends and bringing the kids, which was great, as I got and still do see my kids most weekends. Kelly and Simon are engaged. Our divorce hasn't come through yet, so they haven't set a date. I think they plan on setting up base here, which will mean Amber will be here full time. The teenagers will stay and board at their school. Rachel finishes school in another three months and will be off to college, whilst Gemma still has another year. They both have boyfriends now so they're happy.

Kelly seems to be happy, and she loves Amsterdam as much as me. We meet for coffee once in a while as we really do get on. In fact I've told her about some of my sexploits. Her eyes light up every time.

As for Penny, she still has her safe house for the girls. She has someone else in charge, and she also retired from the window to work on www.pennysnowonline.com. Now she just pops in to make sure everything's ok.

We moved to a fantastic place. We have a disco room with a bar, we have a playroom with fantasy clothing wear and props, and we have a mirrored room with mirrors on the ceiling and mirrors on the walls. It's a great room for having sex in. I love sex, that's something that I found out, and I did find out what my ultimate fantasy is. That's another reason for the trip. We are going to end up doing my ultimate fantasy, so all in all I would say it's a happy ending for all those concerned.

Now you didn't think I was going to leave you like this, with everything hunky dory did you? That would be no fun and no reason to read the next journey, so I'm going to leave you with a little cliffhanger. I know everybody hates a cliffhanger, but it's my story.

Remember that night back in London at the masquerade ball with Penny, and the element of surprise? Penny's rape fantasy? Well what about this for a surprise?

In all the six months I have never been to Penny's place. Then today, of all days, Penny asks me a favor. She is busy with the designer designing a new sexy outfit for pennysnowonline.com.

She needed a book that she left there the last time she visited. The book had some drawings that she wanted to show the designer. Penny tells me to open the door and not to go into any of the rooms apart from the room on the left-hand side. I do exactly that as I'm not going to break Penny's trust.

"The book should just be sitting on the mantlepiece by the wood former not the electric fire that is at the end of the room."

The room is huge and beautifully designed so I go over to the wooden fire and on top there is a book. I pick up the book and there is also a photo frame, glass down so you cannot see the picture. I pick the picture up and turn it around to face me, and staring me bang in the face, is *two Penny Snows*.

That's right. Penny Snow has an identical twin sister. I haven't confronted Penny yet, but it has got me thinking about that night in London. It wasn't Penny I was fucking; it must have been her twin. I leave Penny's place with the book and the photo frame, and make my way back to the apartment to confront Penny.

A sneak peek from the second book

A Fortnight Later

Chapter One
Live Fantasy Auction

So I thought I would wet your appetite a bit more and give you the first chapter of the second book with another twist.

On the same day…

I didn't get a chance to confront Penny about the picture as something came up that needed my attention right away, something that led me away from Amsterdam and back to London.

As I was leaving Penny's place, I got a phone call from Tony, you remember him, right? My best friend, we have been friends since we were 11. We went through high school together, even college until I dropped out. He was my best man at my wedding, he is godfather to the girls, and he is the one person in the whole wide world that has been there for me. He is more than a best friend he is like my brother. We have been through so much together. When I get his phone call asking me for help, I didn't even hesitate, why would I?

I know what I'm about to tell you must sound like the silliest thing in the world but it's what happened and it's what Tony asked me to do.

"Hi Mike, I'm sorry to bother you mate. I know you're about to embark on your travels with Penny, but something has come up and I really need your help. You know I wouldn't ask if it wasn't important, right?"

"Right, go on," I say. "I'm not liking the sound of this, Tone."

"I'm in trouble; big trouble, sort of prison trouble, if I don't do this.   Basically the woman will press charges if you don't do this."

"You are not making any sense, Tony."

"Work has been so slow Mike, that last month I nearly didn't reach my mortgage payment for the house.   Anyway I have been remodeling the inside of this really posh chick's house in Chelsea. The woman is loaded, Mike.   You should see the house, the car, the coats, the bags, the shoes…"

"Yes, yes," I say, "just hurry up and get to the point."

"Well it was Friday.   She always paid me on the last day of the month that fell on a Friday, and I always paid the boys on a Friday.   But two weeks ago she didn't pay me.   She owed me at least 50k, Mike. And the reason for her not paying was because she couldn't be bothered to write the cheque, as she had a dinner function to go to.   Can you believe it? A bloody dinner function!   I have never heard anything so ridiculous in my life, have you Mike?"

"Nope, I can't say I have."

"I had bills to pay, the boys to pay, and I wasn't thinking. I saw her chequebook and opened it, she had already made out the cheque for 50.000 pounds but she hadn't signed it though.   I put a one in front of the 50.000, so it read one hundred and fifty thousand pounds, and put it in my bank.   I know it was stupid…"

"You don't say, Tony! Why didn't you ask me for the money?"

"I don't know Mikey, I don't know."

"So have you been arrested?"

"No I haven't, that's the fucked up thing. When she found out she told me that I must give the money back, of course, and that she won't go to the police if I agree to be in her Live Fantasy Auction."

"What the hell is that? That sounds completely fucked up."

"Tell me about it. Basically she has a load of rich women millionaires, billionaires who are widowed or divorced. Every two weeks she holds an auction with three men and a room full of women bid for the guys. Obviously it's one big cat fight, as there is only three guys to 20 women, so the highest bidder takes home the prize."

"So where do I come into this Tony?"

"Well I was playing football with the lads from the pub. Dean tackled me and I fell hard to the ground. Now I'm all strapped up with a broken leg and broken ankle."

"I still don't understand what that has got to do with me."

"Well the old bitch doesn't want someone with a broken leg. She said I'm useless and will not be able to meet her needs, so the deal is off and she is going to press charges. That was until I said 'well why don't I find a replacement?' I asked a few of the lads in the pub, a lot of them were up for it of course; but no, they didn't quite cut it. She saw a picture of you on my phone and wants you. She wants you to be in her live fantasy auction, and she won't take no for an answer. 'Him or prison' was her exact words."

"Jesus! No way Tony! There must be another way. Let's offer her more money."

"Believe you me Mike, I have tried everything. You name it I've done it. It's the only way to keep me out of prison. The auction is at midday today so you have time to jump on a plane, come to the auction and make it back in time for your trip. I promise Mike."

"It's 10 am now, Tony."

"I know. If you get the 11 am flight it will mean you arrive back in London at 10 am still."

"Thank you Tony. I am aware of the time difference between London and Amsterdam." I pause for a few seconds. "Ok, Ok," I say, "but don't you ever say I do nothing for you. You owe me big time! I will call Dick now."

I ring Dick to take me to the airport. I also ring Penny but her phone goes to voicemail, l so I just tell her something had come up with Tony and I was sorting it but I wouldn't be back at the apartment until at least three or four o'clock.

I rush to the airport and just about make the 11 am flight. Tony has a driver meeting me at the other end that will take me to the Auction, wait, and then take me back to the airport. I arrive at Heathrow 30 minutes late, rush through immigration and see Tony on crutches. "Thank goodness you're here. I thought you were not coming."

"I wouldn't do that to you Tone. So where are we going?"

"The Chelsea Arts Club is where they are holding the auctions.

"I have to tell you Tony, this is sick, don't you think?"

"Well apparently it is all the rage these days. Everybody is having auction dates. There is a big one called *Dinner for Dollars,* it's a fun way for singles to mingle, boom boom."

"Very funny! NOT! Tony, I'm really not in the mood for jokes, let's just get this over and done with. And please, the next time you think about doing anything remotely stupid, call me first."

"Ok boss."

We arrive at the Chelsea Arts Club to be greeted by an awfully posh lady. Not bad looking at all. Sort of has Elizabeth Taylor features about her, her hair in particular.

"Oh thank goodness," she says. "You have arrived. Why are you so late? Oh never mind the excuses, the auction is about to start. Quickly follow me."

Tony hobbles along behind us as fast as he can.

"Right. Here we are," she says. Her voice is very posh English. It is very high-pitched and very annoying. "As you were late, you now cannot choose the fantasy lineup," she says really fast without taking a breath.

And at the end of speaking she stares at me, straight in the face, actually in the eyes, which is so uncomfortable. Her eyes light up, they are opened really wide and she pouts her lips and just stares at me. I don't know what to do. I feel like a schoolboy getting told off. It's like she is waiting for a sorry or some type of answer from me.

"Ok, blonde boy has the picture frame. Italian has the fruit, so that leaves… um, oh yes, that leaves the butler."

"The what?" I say. She ignores me.

"Take your clothes off. Fully strip down butt naked, please."

"I beg your pardon." Again she ignores me.

Tony whispers, "Just do it. The quicker it is done, the quicker we get out of here."

"Easy for you to say, you're not butt naked." I take all my clothes off, even my watch and my socks and hand them to her.

"Phone and wallet," she says.

"There in my coat," I say. She dumps my clothes into a bin, takes my phone and wallet out of my coat and puts them into her Mary Poppins style bag. I'm standing there butt naked, with my hand covering my private parts.

"Oh no," she says, "you don't need to use your hands." She passes me a silver tray. "The butler," she says. Ok, I get it now; I'm a naked butler. She then puts a collar around my neck.

"Very nice, very nice indeed. Come along," in that awful high-pitched voice, "it's started." She prods me with her skinny finger in the arm, "This way, follow me."

We walk out of the dressing room up some stairs and I find myself at the side of the stage. The blonde guy is on the stage; he is holding a photo frame that is covering his bits. He is turning around so the women can see his bum. He is taking it all in and loving it. I then get a glimpse of the crowd: all women, old women, young women, fat women all heckling, and shouting obscene amounts of money. Close your eyes and imagine the scene out of the movie *Snatch* when they are bare knuckle fighting, that's what this was like but worse. Gosh my head is spinning.

The auctioneer lady also is a very odd looking character, like something dated from the Victorian days. In fact, she does look like a Victorian widow with her black lace covering her face.

"So who is going to start this bid off?"

"I do," a rather big lady says.

"5000 pounds do I hear?"

Another lady shouts, "five thousand, five hundred."

"Five thousand eight hundred." Another lady.

"Eight thousand," says another lady.

It goes on and on, the women now are like cackling hens.

"Ok going once, going twice, sold to the lady in the green for 15000 pounds."

Jesus, 15,000 pounds for him. This is not real this is twisted shit.

"And next up we have the fruit platter. Are any of you ladies feeling fruity today? Then here is your man." Out walks the Italian guy, he is very good looking and has a great muscular body. He is covering his bits with an apple and banana.

"Let the bidding commence." A little lady with bright red hair shouts out "10000 pounds". The bids then go up in increments of 5'000 until the final hammer hits down on 30000 pounds. This is ludicrous! Have these women got more money then sense? Obviously they do. Surely they should be buying fur coats and handbags.

"Sold to the lady in the orange hat." I feel so sorry for him. The lady who won him was a very large lady, she looks like an orange herself.

"Now for the last bid of the day. We all need waiting on ladies, so here is your chance."

"Out, out you go," she prods me. I walk onto the stage, really nervous. There is a big spotlight on me that blinds me; I lift my hands to shield the light, forgetting that I have a tray covering me up. The tray falls to the floor with an almighty bang, and all the women start laughing. I just stand there looking at their cackling faces hoping that I don't get the really old lady at the front of the stage that is already waving her hands furiously. I pick up the tray cover, back up and just zone out.

The next minute I'm being pulled of the stage by the voice. "Oh, congratulations! You got the biggest bid today of 100,000 pounds and you have been sold to our very own hostess of the event, Mrs. Wilkins. She has already left. You are to be driven straight to her house. Here is a personal note from her."

> Hello.
>
> I paid a lot of money to get you. So many women wanted you, especially when they saw what you have down there. You are to be mine, my possession for the next two weeks, to do with you as I please, mentally, physically and sexually.
>
> And before you get any ideas of absconding, remember your friend and his unfortunate altercation. For safe measures the collar you have around your neck is an electric collar, which will electrocute you.
>
> See you soon my darling. The car is waiting right outside. Make sure you get into the right car. It's the Bentley.

I touch my neck and feel the collar. I try and take it off and it electrocutes me. I fall on the floor I'm in so much pain. The electric shock shoots through my whole body that it takes the wind from me.

About The Author

Eddie Bean (pseudonym) hails from the UK and has recently moved to Los Angeles. Bean is a former adult movie director and writer for an adult men's magazine *Club DVD*.

Married to someone famous with two children, Bean has now decided the time has come to tell the story of all the sexual experiences and fantasies that have happened over the years.

www.ingramcontent.com/pod-product-compliance
Lightning Source LLC
Chambersburg PA
CBHW070916130626
46555CB00001B/158